THE SOCIALITE AND THE CATTLE KING

BY
LINDSAY ARMSTRONG

MILLS
BOON

DID YOU PURCHASE THIS BOOK WITHOUT A COVER?

If you did, you should be aware it is **stolen property** as it was reported *unsold and destroyed* by a retailer. Neither the author nor the publisher has received any payment for this book.

All the characters in this book have no existence outside the imagination of the author, and have no relation whatsoever to anyone bearing the same name or names. They are not even distantly inspired by any individual known or unknown to the author, and all the incidents are pure invention.

All Rights Reserved including the right of reproduction in whole or in part in any form. This edition is published by arrangement with Harlequin Enterprises II BV/S.à.r.l. The text of this publication or any part thereof may not be reproduced or transmitted in any form or by any means, electronic or mechanical, including photocopying, recording, storage in an information retrieval system, or otherwise, without the written permission of the publisher.

This book is sold subject to the condition that it shall not, by way of trade or otherwise, be lent, resold, hired out or otherwise circulated without the prior consent of the publisher in any form of binding or cover other than that in which it is published and without a similar condition including this condition being imposed on the subsequent purchaser.

® and TM are trademarks owned and used by the trademark owner and/or its licensee. Trademarks marked with ® are registered with the United Kingdom Patent Office and/or the Office for Harmonisation in the Internal Market and in other countries.

First published in Great Britain 2010
Harlequin Mills & Boon Limited,
Eton House, 18-24 Paradise Road, Richmond, Surrey TW9 1SR

© Lindsay Armstrong 2010

ISBN: 978 0 263 87860 8

Harlequin Mills & Boon policy is to use papers that are natural, renewable and recyclable products and made from wood grown in sustainable forests. The logging and manufacturing process conform to the legal environmental regulations of the country of origin.

Printed and bound in Spain
by Litografia Rosés, S.A., Barcelona

THE SOCIALITE
AND THE
CATTLE KING

BIRMINGHAM LIBRARIES

ACOCKS GREEN

ACOCKS GREEN

CHAPTER ONE

HOLLY HARDING had the world at her feet—or she should have had.

The only child of wealthy parents—although her father had died—she could have rested on her laurels and fulfilled her mother's dearest ambition for her, that she settle down and make an appropriate, although of course happy, marriage.

Holly, however, had other ideas. Not that she was against wedlock in general, but she knew she wasn't ready for it. Sometimes she doubted she ever would be, but she went out of her way not to dwell on the reason for that...

Instead, she concentrated on her career. She was a journalist, although occasionally she partook of the social scene so dear to her mother's heart; Sylvia Harding was a well-known socialite. It was on two such occasions that Holly had encountered Brett Wyndham, with disastrous consequences.

'A masked fancy-dress ball and a charity lunch? You must be out of your mind,' Brett Wyndham said to his sister Sue.

He'd just flown in from India, on a delayed flight that

had also been diverted, so he was tired and irritable. His sister's plans for his social life did not appear to improve his mood.

'Oh, they're not so bad,' Sue said. She was in her late twenties, dark-haired like her brother, but petite and pretty—quite unlike her brother. She was also looking a bit pale and strained, whilst trying to strike an enthusiastic note. 'And it is a good cause—the lunch, anyway. What's wrong with raising money for animal shelters? I thought that might appeal to you. I mean, I know they may only be cats and dogs...'

Brett said wearily, 'I can't stand them. I can't stand the food, I can't stand the women—'

'The women?' Sue interrupted with a frown. 'You don't usually have a problem there. What's wrong with them?'

Brett opened his mouth to say, *They are usually the most ferociously groomed set of women you've ever seen in your life, from their dyed hair, their fake eyelashes, their plucked eyebrows, their fake nails and tans; they're ghastly.* But he didn't say it. Although she didn't have a fake tan or fake eyelashes, his sister was exquisitely groomed and most expensively dressed.

He shrugged. 'Their perfume alone is enough to give me hay fever,' he said moodily instead. 'And, honestly, I have a problem with the concept of turning fund-raising into society events that bring out all the social climbers and publicity seekers.' He stopped and shook his head.

'Brett, please!'

But Brett Wyndham was not to be placated. 'As for masked fancy-dress balls,' he went on, 'I can't stand the fools men make of themselves. And the women; something about being disguised, or thinking they are, seems to bring out the worst in them.'

'What do you mean?'

'I mean, beloved,' he said dryly, 'They develop almost predator-like tendencies.' For the first time a glint of humour lit his dark eyes. 'You need to be particularly careful or you can find yourself shackled, roped and on the way to the altar.'

Sue smiled. 'I don't think you would ever have that problem.'

He shrugged. 'Then there's Mark and Aria's wedding coming up shortly—the reason I'm home, anyway.' Mark was their brother. 'I've no idea what's planned but I'm sure there'll be plenty of partying involved.'

Sue's smile faded as she nodded, and tears came to her eyes.

Brett frowned down at her. 'Susie? What's wrong?'

'I've left Brendan.' Brendan was her husband of three years. 'I found out he was being unfaithful to me.'

Brett closed his eyes briefly. He could have said, *I told you so*, but he didn't. He put his arms around his sister instead.

'You were right about him.' Sue wept. 'I think all he was after was my money.'

'I guess we have to make our own mistakes.'

'Yes, but I feel so stupid. And—' she gulped back some tears '—I feel everyone must be laughing at me. Apparently it was no big secret. I was the last person to know,' she said tragically.

'It's often the way.'

'It may be, but it doesn't make it any easier.'

'Are you still in love with him?' Brett queried.

'No! Well, how could I be?'

Brett smiled absently.

'But one thing I do know,' Sue said with utter conviction. 'I refuse to go into a decline, I refuse to run away and hide and I refuse to be a laughing stock!'

'Susie—'

But his sister overrode him, with tears in her eyes still, but determination too. 'I'm patron of the Animal Shelter Society so I will be at the lunch. The ball is one of the festivities planned for the Winter Racing Carnival; I'm on the committee, so I'll be there too, and I'll make sure everyone knows who I am! But—' she sagged a little against him 'I—would dearly love some moral support.'

'I beg your pardon?' Mike Rafferty said to his boss, Brett Wyndham.

They were in Brett's apartment high above the Brisbane River and the elegant curves of the William Jolly Bridge. Sue, who'd insisted on picking him up from the airport, had just left.

'You heard,' Brett replied shortly.

'Well, I thought I did. You asked me to make a note of the fact that you were going to a charity lunch tomorrow and a masked fancy-dress ball on Friday night. I just couldn't believe my ears.'

'Don't make too big a thing of this, Mike,' Brett warned. 'I'm not in the mood.'

'Of course not. They could even be—quite enjoyable.'

Brett cast him a dark glance and got up to walk over

to the window with his familiar long-legged prowl. With his short, ruffled dark hair, blue shadows on his jaw, a kind of eagle intensity about his dark eyes, his cargo pants and black sweatshirt, his height and broad shoulders, he could have been anything.

What did come to mind was a trained-to-perfection daredevil member of a SWAT team.

In fact, Brett Wyndham was a vet and he specialized in saving endangered species, the more dangerous the better, such as the black rhino, elephants and tigers.

He dropped out of helicopters with tranquilizer guns, he parachuted into jungles—all in a day's work. He also managed the family fortunes that included some huge cattle-stations, and since he'd taken over the reins of the Wyndham empire he'd tripled that fortune so he was now a billionaire, although a very reclusive one. He did not give interviews but word of his work had filtered out and he'd captured the public's imagination.

As Brett's PA, it fell to Mike Rafferty to ensure his privacy here in Brisbane, amongst other duties at Haywire—one of the cattle stations in Far North Queensland the Wyndham dynasty called home—and at Palm Cove where they owned a resort.

'So will you be saying anything to the press?' he queried. 'There's bound to be some coverage of the lunch tomorrow, even if you'll be incognito at the ball.'

'No. I'm not saying anything to anyone although, according to my sister, my presence alone will invest the proceedings with quite some clout.' He grimaced.

'It probably will,' Mike agreed. 'And what will you be going to the masked ball as?'

'I have no idea. I'll leave that up to you—but

something discreet, Mike,' Brett growled. 'No monkey suit, no toga and laurel wreath, no Tarzan or *anything* like that.' He stopped and yawned. 'And now I'm going to bed.'

'Mum,' Holly said to her mother the next morning, 'I'm not sure about this outfit. Isn't the lunch supposed to be a fundraiser?' She glanced down at herself. She wore a fitted little black jacket with a low vee-neck over a very short black-and-white skirt. Black high-heeled sandals exposed newly painted pink toenails, matching her fingernails. She wore her mother's pearl choker and matching pendant earrings.

'It certainly is,' Sylvia replied. 'And a very exclusive one. The tickets cost a fortune, although of course they are tax deductible,' she assured her daughter. 'But you look stunning, darling!'

Holly grimaced and twirled in front of the mirror. They were in her bedroom in the family home, a lovely old house high on a hill in Balmoral. She still lived at home, or rather had moved back in after her father had died to keep her mother company. There were plenty of advantages to this arrangement that Holly was most appreciative of, which was why she humoured her mother now and then and attended these kinds of function.

Quite how she'd got roped into going to a charity lunch and a masked fancy-dress ball within a few days of each other she wasn't sure, but she knew it did give her mother a lot of pleasure to have her company. It also gave her a lot of pleasure to dress her daughter up to the nines.

Holly was quite tall and very slim, two things that

lent themselves to wearing clothes well, although when left to her own devices she favoured 'very casual'. She herself thought her looks were unexceptional, although she did have deep-blue eyes and a thick cloud of fair but hard-to-manage hair.

Today her hair was up in an elaborate chignon, and sprayed and pinned within in inch of its life to stay that way. Sylvia's hairdresser, who made house calls, had also done their nails.

Sylvia herself was resplendent in diamonds and a fuchsia linen suit.

Despite her mother's preoccupation with the social scene, Holly loved Sylvia and felt for her in her loneliness now she was a widow. But the most formative person in Holly's life had been her father, imbuing her not only with his love of the different but his love of writing.

Richard Harding, had he been born in another era, would have been a Dr Livingstone or Mr Stanley. He'd inherited considerable means and had loved nothing better than to travel, to explore out-of-the-way places and different cultures, and to write about them. The fact that he'd married someone almost the exact opposite had been something of a mystery to Holly, yet when they'd been together her parents had been happy.

But it was Holly who Richard had taken more and more on his expeditions. Amongst the results for Holly had been a well-rounded informal education alongside her formal one and fluency in French, plus some Spanish and a smattering of Swahili.

All of it had contributed towards Holly's present job. She was a travel reporter for an upmarket magazine but with a slight difference: hard-to-get-to places were her speciality. As a consequence, to bring to life her destinations, she'd used bad-tempered camels, stubborn donkeys, dangerous-looking vehicles driven by manic individuals and overcrowded ferries.

According to her editor, Glenn Shepherd, she might look as if a good puff of wind would blow her away but she had a hint of inner steel. She had to, to have coped with some of the situations she'd landed herself in.

She'd shrugged when he'd said this to her and had responded, 'Oh, I don't know. Sometimes looking and playing dumb works wonders.'

He'd grinned at her. 'What about the sheikh fellow who introduced you to all his wives with a view to you joining the clan? Or the Mexican bandit who wanted to marry you?'

'Ah, that required a bit of ingenuity. I actually had to steal his vehicle,' Holly had confessed. 'But I did have it returned to him. Glenn, I've been doing travel for a couple of years now—any chance of a change?'

'Thought you loved it?'

'I do, but I also want to spread my wings journalistically. I'd love to be given something I could *investigate* or someone I could get the definitive interview from.'

Glenn had sat forward. 'Holly, I'm not saying you're not capable of it, but you are only twenty-four; some kinds of—insight, I guess, take a bit longer than that to develop. It will come, but keep up the good work in the meantime. More and more people out there are getting to love your pieces. Also, re the definitive interview, we have a policy; any of our staff can try for one, so long as they pull it off ethically, and if it's good enough we'll publish it. But I must warn you, it has to be outstanding.'

'As in?'

'Mostly as in, well, surprise factor.' He'd shrugged. 'Brett Wyndham, for example.'

Holly had grimaced. 'That's like asking for the moon.'

Holly came back to the present and took one last look at herself. 'If you're sure,' she said to her mother, 'We're not terribly over-dressed?'

'We're not,' Sylvia said simply.

Holly saw that she was right when she took her place in the upmarket Milton restaurant that had been turned into a tropical greenhouse. She was amidst a noisy throng of very upmarket-looking guests. Almost without exception, the women were exquisitely groomed, expensively dressed and their jewellery flashed beneath the overhead lighting; many of them wore hats. Not only that, a lot of them seemed to know each other, so it was a convivial gathering helped along by the wine that started to flow. Recent cruises, skiing holidays and tropical islands featured in the snippets of conversation Holly heard around her, as well as the difficulties attached to finding really good housekeepers.

There were men present but they were rather outnumbered. One of them took his place beside Holly.

Goodness, gracious me! was Holly's first, startled reaction.

The man who sat down beside her was tall and beautifully proportioned; he was dark and satanic looking. He had a suppressed air of vitality combined with an arrogance that was repressed, but nevertheless you couldn't help but know it was there in the tilt of his head and the set of his mouth. All in all he made the little hairs on her arms stand up in a way that made her blink.

He was casually dressed in khaki trousers, a sports jacket and a navy-blue shirt. He looked out moodily over the assembled throng then concentrated on the first speaker of the day.

The patron of the shelter society introduced herself as Sue Murray. She was petite and dark, and clearly under some strain, as she stumbled a couple of times, then looked straight at the man beside Holly, drew a deep breath, and continued her speech smoothly. She gave a short résumé of the shelter society's activities and plans for the future, then she thanked everyone for coming. There was loud applause as she stepped down.

'Poor thing,' Sylvia whispered into Holly's ear. 'Her husband's been playing around. Darling, would you mind if I popped over to another table? I've just spied an old friend I haven't seen for ages. I'll be back when they start serving lunch.'

'Of course not,' Holly whispered back, and turned automatically to the man beside her as she unfolded her napkin. The seat on the other side of him was empty too, so they were like a little island in the throng. 'How do you do?'

'How do you do?' he replied coolly and studied all he could see of her, from her upswept hair, her pearls, the vee between her breasts exposed by her jacket and her slim waist. But it was worse than that. She got the distinct feeling he was viewing her without her clothes and with a view to assessing her potential as a partner in his bed.

She lowered her lashes swiftly as her blue eyes blazed at the sheer insolence of this unexpected appraisal, and at the inexplicable reaction it aroused in her. A wholly unexpected ripple of awareness touched her nerve ends.

Her lips parted on a stinging retort, but before she could frame it he smiled slightly, a lethally insolent twisting of his lips as if he was quite aware of his effect on her, and posed a question to her with an air of patent scepticism.

'Are you a great supporter of animal shelters?'

Holly looked taken aback for a moment but she recovered swiftly and said, 'No—not that I'm against them.' She shrugged. 'But that's not why I'm here.'

His eyes left her face briefly and she realized he was keeping tabs on the progress of Sue Murray as she moved from table to table introducing herself to everyone. When his gaze came back to her, he posed another question. 'Why *are* you here?'

'I came with my mother.'

A glint of amusement lit his dark eyes. 'That sounds as if it came from a list of excuses the Department of Transport publishes occasionally: "my mother told me to hurry up, that's why I was exceeding the speed limit".'

If she hadn't been so annoyed, if it hadn't been so apt, Holly would have seen the humour of this.

'Clever,' she said coldly. 'But I have to tell you, I'm already regretting it. And, for your further information, I don't approve of this kind of fund-raising.'

He lifted a lazy eyebrow. 'Strange, that. You look so very much the part.'

'What *part*?' she asked arctically.

He shrugged. 'The professional, serial socialite. The embodiment of conspicuous philanthropy in order to climb the social ladder.' He glanced at her left hand, which happened to be bare of rings. 'Maybe even in the market for a rich husband?' he added with soft but lethal irony.

Holly gasped, and gasped again, as his gaze flickered over her and came back to rest squarely on her décolletage; she had no doubt that he was mentally undressing her.

Then she clenched her teeth as it crossed her mind that she should have stuck to her guns. She should not be sitting there all dolled up to the nines, with her hair strangled up and starting to give her a headache, all to support a cause but giving off the wrong messages entirely. Obviously!

On the other hand, she thought swiftly, that did not give this man the right to insult her.

'If you'll forgive me for saying so,' she retorted, 'I think your manners are atrocious.'

'Oh. In what way?'

'How or why I'm here has nothing whatsoever to do with you and if you mentally undress me once more who knows what I might be prompted to do? I am,' she added, 'quite able to take care of myself, and I'm not wet behind the ears.'

'Fighting words,' he murmured. 'But there is this—'

'I know what you're going to say,' she broke in. 'It's

chemistry.' She looked at him scornfully. 'That is such an old, dead one! Even my Mexican bandit didn't use that one although, come to think of it, the sheikh did. Well, I think that's what he was saying.' She tipped her hand as if to say, 'you win some, you lose some'.

He blinked. 'Sounds as if you have an interesting life.'

'I do.'

'You're not making it all up?'

'No.' Holly folded her arms and waited.

'What?' he queried after a moment, with utterly false trepidation.

'I thought an apology might be appropriate.'

He said nothing, just gazed at her, and after a pensive moment on her part they were exchanging a long, telling look which came as quite a surprise to Holly. The luncheon and its environs receded and it was if there was only the two of them...

Whatever was happening for him, for Holly it became a drawing-in, not only visually but through her pores, of the essence of this man and the acknowledgement that his physical properties were extremely fine. He was not only tall, he was tanned, and he looked exceedingly fit, as if sitting at charity luncheons did not come naturally to him. His hands were long and well-shaped. His dark hair was crisp and short, and the lines and angles of his face were interesting but not easy to read.

In fact, she summarized to herself, there was something inherently dangerous but dynamically attractive about him that made you think of him having his hands on your body, his exciting, expert, mind-blowing way with you.

That's ridiculous, she told herself as a strange little thrill ran through her. *That's such a* girlish *fantasy!*

Nevertheless, it continued to do strange things to her.

It altered the rate of her breathing, for example. It caused a little pulse to beat rather wildly at the base of her throat so that her pearls jumped. To her amazement, it even caused her nipples to become sensitive and make the lace of her black bra feel almost intolerably scratchy.

Her lips parted, then she made a concerted attempt to gather her composure as his dark gaze raked her again, but he broke the spell.

He said very quietly, 'I don't know about the bandit or the sheikh, ma'am, but I can't help thinking chemistry is actually alive and well—between us.'

Holly came back to earth with a thud and rose to her feet. 'I'm leaving,' she said baldly.

He sat back and shrugged. 'Please don't on my account. I'll say no more. Anyway, what about your mother?' he queried with just a shadow of disbelief.

Holly looked around a little wildly. 'I'll take her with me. Yes!' And she strode away from the table.

'I'm sorry, I'm so sorry,' Holly said as she clutched the steering wheel and started to drive them home. Her mother still looked stunned. 'But he was—impossible, the man sitting next to me! Talk about making a pass!' she marvelled.

'Brett Wyndham made a pass at you?' Sylvia said in faint accents as she clutched the arm rest. 'Holly, slow down, darling!'

Holly did more, she stamped on the brakes then pulled off the road. 'Brett Wyndham,' she repeated incredulously. '*That* was Brett Wyndham?'

'Yes. Sue Murray's his sister. We can only assume that's why he's there. I told you, she's having husband troubles, and perhaps he's providing moral support or something like that. I've never seen him at such a function before, or any kind of function for that matter.'

Holly released the wheel and clutched her head, then she started shedding hairpins haphazardly into her lap. 'If only I'd known! But would I have done anything differently? He was exceedingly—he was— That's why he was watching her.'

'Who?'

'His sister. In between watching me,' Holly said bitterly. 'On the other hand, I could maybe have seen the funny side of it. I could have deflected him humorously and—who knows?'

'If I had the faintest idea what you were talking about I might be able to agree or disagree,' her mother said plaintively.

Holly turned to her then hugged her. 'I am sorry. On all counts. And don't mind me; it's just that an interview with Brett Wyndham could have been the real boost my career needs.'

CHAPTER TWO

A COUPLE of days later, Holly found she couldn't get out of the masked fancy-dress ball she'd agreed to attend with her mother, much as she would have loved to.

When she raised the matter, Sylvia pointed out that it would make the table numbers uneven, for one thing, and for another wasn't her costume inspired—especially for a girl called Holly?

'So, who are we going with?' Holly queried.

'Two married couples and a gentleman friend of mind, plus his son: a nice table of eight,' Sylvia said contentedly.

Holly had met the gentleman friend, a widower, but not the son. In answer to her query on that subject, she received the news that the son was only twenty-one but a very nice, mature boy. Holly digested this information with inward scepticism. 'Mature and twenty-one' in young men did not always go together, in her opinion, but then she consoled herself with the thought that her mother couldn't have any expectations of a twenty-one-year-old as in husband material for Holly, surely?

Still, she wasn't brimming with keenness to go—but she remembered how she'd probably embarrassed the life out of her mother a few days ago, and she decided to bite the bullet.

Unfortunately, the memory of the lunch brought Brett Wyndham back to mind and demonstrated to her that she didn't have an unequivocal stance on the memory. Yes, she'd been outraged at his approach at the time—who wouldn't have been? He'd accused her of being a serial socialite and a gold-digger.

Of course, there'd been an intrinsic undercurrent to that in his own fairly obvious distaste for the lunch and all it stood for. Why else would he challenge her motives for being there? But—another but—how did that fit in with his sister being the patron of the shelter society?

Ironic, however, was the fact that two things had chipped away at her absolute outrage, making it not quite so severe: the undoubted frisson he'd aroused in her being one. Put simply, it translated into the fact that he'd been the first man to excite her physically since, well, in quite a long time...

She looked into the distance and shivered before bringing herself back to the present and forcing herself to face the second factor that had slightly lessened her outrage. Had she mucked up a golden opportunity to get the interview that would have boosted her career?

Yes, she answered herself, well and truly mucked it up. But there was no way she would have done anything differently so she just had to live with it!

All the same, militant as she felt on the subject of Brett Wyndham on one hand, on the other she had an impulse, one that actually made her fingers itch—to look him up on the Internet.

She shook her head and fought it but it was a fight

she lost, and her fingers flew over the keys of her laptop, only to find that not a lot personal came to light. He was thirty-five, the oldest of three. There was a brother between him and his sister Sue, a brother who was getting married shortly. In fact, there was more about this brother Mark, his fiancée Aria and Sue Murray than there was about Brett Wyndham, so far as personal lives went.

She dug a bit further and established that the Wyndhams had been pioneers in the savannah country of Far North Queensland where they'd established their cattle stations. She learnt that Haywire, situated between Georgetown and Croydon, was the station they called home. And she learnt that the red-basalt soil in the area produced grass that cattle thrived upon—quite beside the point. Well, the treacherous little thought crept into her mind, not so much beside the point if she ever got to interview the man!

She also learnt that Brett Wyndham was a powerful figure in other ways. The empire was no longer based solely on pastoralism. He had mining interests in the area, marble from Chillagoe, zinc and transport companies. He employed a significant amount of people in these enterprises, and he was respected for his environmental views, as well as views on endangered species.

Then she turned up gold, from her point of view—a rather bitchy little article about one Natasha Hewson, who was described as extraordinarily beautiful and extremely talented. Apparently she ran an agency that specialized in organizing events and functions down to the last exquisite detail for the rich and famous. But, the article went on to say, if Natasha had hoped to be last in the long line of beautiful women Brett Wyndham had squired when they'd got engaged, her hopes had been dashed when they'd broken off the engagement recently...

Holly checked the date and saw that it was only nine months ago.

She sat back and tapped her teeth with the end of her pen. She had to admit that he'd got to her in a way that had reawakened her from a couple of years of mental and physical celibacy—but had she wanted to be re-awakened? Not by a man who could have any woman he wanted, and had had a long line of them, she thought swiftly.

Mind you—she smiled a rueful smile—there was no hope of her getting an interview with him anyway, so it was best just to forget it all.

Brett Wyndham wondered how soon he'd be able to leave the ball. He'd come partnerless—well, he'd come with his sister. True to her word, she was looking stunning in a lavender crinoline, but otherwise apart from her tiny mask was quite recognizable as Sue Murray. Moreover she was putting a brave face on even if her heart was breaking and, whether it was his presence or not, no-one appeared to be making a laughing stock of her.

He watched her dance past—he'd left their table and was standing at the bar—and he found himself pondering the nature of love. Sue felt she shouldn't be able to love Brendan Murray now but was that all it took in matters of the heart? Dictating to yourself what you should or should not feel?

Which led him in turn to ponder his own love life. The nature of his life seemed to ensure that the women in it were only passing companions, but there had been no shortage of them. The problem was, he couldn't seem to drum up much enthusiasm for any of them.

Not only that, perhaps it was the inability of those partners to disguise their expectations that he was getting tired of, he reflected. Or the fact that none of them ever said 'no.' Well, one had quite recently, now he came to think of it. His lips twisted with amusement at the memory.

He shrugged and turned to watch the passing parade.

He'd come, courtesy of Mike Rafferty, as a masked Spanish aristocrat with a dark cropped jacket, dark, trousers, soft boots and white, frilled shirt, complete with scarlet cummerbund and black felt hat.

Dinner was over and the serious part of the evening under way—the serious dancing, that was. They were all there, strutting their stuff to the powerful beat of the music under the chandelier: the Cleopatras, the Marie Antoinettes, the belly dancers, the harem girls, the Lone Rangers, the Lawrences of Arabia, the three Elvises, a Joan of Arc and a Lady Godiva in a body stocking who looked as if she was regretting her choice of costume.

Some of them he recognized despite the masks and towering wigs. All of them, he reflected, bored him to tears.

He was just about to turn away when one girl he didn't recognize danced past in the arms of an eager pirate complete with eye patch, one gold earring and a stuffed macaw on his shoulder.

She was quite tall, very slim and dressed almost all in black. Something about her, probably her outfit, stirred something in his memory, but he couldn't pin it down.

'Who's she supposed to be?' he enquired of an elderly milkmaid standing beside him. He indicated the girl in black.

The milkmaid beamed. 'Isn't she perfect? So different. Of course, it's Holly Golightly—don't you remember? Audrey Hepburn in *Breakfast at Tiffany's*. That gorgeous black hat with the wide, downturned brim and the light, floaty hat-band; the earrings, the classic little black dress and gloves—even the alligator shoes. And to think of using her sunglasses as a mask!'

'Ah. Yes, she is rather perfect. You wouldn't happen to know who she is in real life?'

The milkmaid had no idea and Brett watched Holly Golightly dance past again.

She looked cool and detached, even slightly superior, but that could be because the pirate was having trouble containing his enthusiasm for her.

In fact, as he watched she detached herself from her partner as he attempted to maul her, swung on her heel and swept away towards the ballroom balcony with a hand to her hat.

The pirate looked so crestfallen, Brett could only assume he was either very young or very drunk.

Without giving it much thought, he took a fresh glass of champagne off the bar and followed the girl onto the balcony.

She was leaning against the balustrade, breathing deeply.

'Maybe this'll help to remove the taste of the pirate?' he suggested and offered the champagne to her.

Holly straightened and wondered if she was imagining things. She'd been rather darkly contemplating the fact that she'd been right about very young men such as the pirate who was the son of her mother's friend; he hadn't been able to keep his hands off her!

But could this tall, arrogant-looking Spaniard be who she thought he was? Could you ever forget Brett Wyndham's voice, or his athletic build? Or the pass he'd made at her? More importantly, did she want to be recognized? As a serious journalist, perhaps, but like this? As a *serial socialite*…?

In a lightning decision that she did not want to be recognized, she lowered her voice a notch and assumed a French accent. '*Merci*. I was of a mind to punch his parrot.'

Brett laughed then narrowed his eyes behind the mask. 'You sound as if you've just stepped out of France.'

'Not France, Tahiti.' It wasn't exactly a lie. She'd returned from her last travel assignment, Papeete, a bare week ago.

'So, a Tahitian Holly Golightly?'

'You may say so.' Holly sipped some champagne. 'What have we with you? An Aussie *señor*?'

He looked down at his attire. 'You could say so. Are you into horses, Miss Golightly?'

Holly gazed at him blankly.

'It *is* the kick-off to the Winter Racing Carnival, this ball,' he elaborated.

'Of course! But no, you could say not, although I

have done some riding in my time. Generally, though, on inferior beasts such as asses and camels.'

Brett's eyebrows shot up. 'Camels? In Tahiti? How come?'

'Not, naturally, Tahiti,' Holly denied regally. 'But I have a fondness for some out-of-the-way places you cannot get to by *other* means.' She gave the word "other" a tremendous French twist.

'So do I,' he murmured and frowned again as his masked gaze roamed over her.

Holly waited with some trepidation. Would he recognize her beneath the Holly Golightly outfit, the wide, downturned hat-brim and the French accent? She'd recognized him almost immediately, but that deep, mesmerizing voice would be hard to disguise. For that matter, so were those wide shoulders and lean hips.

Then it occurred to her that she was once again being summed up in that inimitable way of his.

The slender line of her neck, the outline of her figure beneath the little black dress, the smooth skin of her arms above her gloves, her trim ankles—they all received his critical assessment. And they all traitorously reacted accordingly, which was to say he might as well have been running his hands over her body.

'Actually,' she said airily—not a true reflection of her emotions as she was battling to stay cool and striving to take a humorous view of proceedings, 'You make a *trés* arrogant Spaniard.'

'I do?'

'*Oui*. Summing up perfectly strange women with a view to ownership is what I would call arrogant. Could it be that there is little difference between you and the pirate with the parrot, *monsieur*?'

'Ownership?' he queried.

'Of their bodies,' she explained. 'Tell me this was not so a moment ago?' She tilted her chin at him.

He pushed his hands into his pockets and shrugged. 'It's a failing most men succumb to. But unlike the pirate I would never attempt to maul you, Miss Golightly.'

He paused and allowed his dark, masked gaze to travel over her again. 'On the contrary, I would make your skin feel like warm silk and I would celebrate your lovely, slim body in a way that would be entirely satisfactory—for both of us.'

Holly stifled a tremor of utmost sensuousness that threatened to engulf her down the length of her body—at least stifled the outward appearance of it, by the narrowest of margins.

All the same, she went hot and cold and had to wonder how he did it. How did he engender a state of mind that could even have her wondering what it would be like to be Brett Wyndham's woman. How dared he?

Despite his arrogance, did that dark, swashbuckling presence do it to most women he came in contact with?

Her mind swooped on this point. Would it be a relief to think she was just one of a crowd when it came to Brett Wyndham? Or would it make it worse?

She came to her senses abruptly to find him studying her intently now and rather differently. 'You have a problem, *señor*?'

'No. Well, I just have the feeling I've met you before, Miss Golightly.'

Holly took the bit between her teeth and contrived a quizzical little smile. 'Many men have that problem. It is a very—how do you say it?—unoriginal approach.'

'You feel I'm making a pass at you?' he enquired lazily.

'I am convinced of it.' She presented him her half empty champagne glass. 'Thus, I will return to my party. *Au revoir.*'

But he said, 'Were you riding a camel when your sheikh propositioned you?'

Holly, in the act of sweeping inside, stopped as if shot.

'Or a donkey, when the Mexican approached you?' he added softly.

'You knew!' she accused.

'The accent and the outfit threw me for a while, but I'm not blind or deaf. Is it *all* made up? And, if so, why?'

Holly walked back to him and retrieved her champagne. 'I've got the feeling I might need this,' she said darkly and took a good sip. 'No, well, Tahiti was true—a bit. I've just come back so it seemed like a good idea to—' she gestured airily '—to...' But she couldn't think of a suitable way to cloak it.

'Help pull the wool over my eyes?' he suggested.

Holly choked slightly on a second sip of champagne but made a swift recovery. 'Why would I want to be recognized by you? All you ever do is query my motives, accuse me of appalling posturing and make passes at me!'

'You have to admit it all sounds highly unlikely,' he drawled. 'Are you here with your mother?'

Holly opened her mouth but closed it and stamped her foot. 'Don't you dare make fun of my mother! She—'

A flash of pale colour registered in her peripheral vision and she turned to see her mother coming out onto the balcony. Her mother was dressed as Eliza Doolittle at the races, complete with huge hat and parasol. 'We might as well both reprise Audrey Hepburn roles,' Sylvia had said upon presenting the idea to her daughter.

'Mum!' Holly said. 'What—'

But her mother interrupted her. 'There you are, darling! And I see you've met Mr Wyndham.' Sylvia turned to Brett. 'How do you do? I'm Sylvia Harding, Holly's mother—yes, her real name is Holly, that's why we thought of Holly Golightly!' Sylvia paused and took a very deep breath. 'But I feel sure there was some misunderstanding at the shelter lunch, and she didn't have the opportunity to tell you that she's a journalist and would love to interview you.'

There was dead silence on the balcony but Sylvia went on, apparently oblivious to the undercurrents. 'I also know she'd do a great job; she's not her father's daughter for nothing. He was Richard Harding, incidentally—perhaps you've heard of him?'

'Yes, I have. How do you do, Mrs Harding?' Brett said courteously.

'I'm fine, thank you. You may be wondering how I recognized you, but as soon as I saw you with Sue it clicked. She's such a lovely person, your sister. Well, I'll leave you two together.' She hesitated then walked back inside.

Holly let out a long breath then finished the champagne with a gulp. 'Don't say a word,' she warned Brett, once again presented him with her glass. 'I did not arrange that, and anyway I don't believe leopards change their spots, so I have no desire to interview you.'

'Leopards?' he queried gravely but she could see he was struggling not to laugh. 'On top of camels, asses, Mexicans and sheikhs?'

'Yes,' she said through her teeth. 'I believe they can be cunning, highly dangerous and thoroughly bad-minded into the bargain. If anyone should know that, you should.'

'I do,' he agreed. 'Uh—where is this analogy leading?'

'I have no faith in you *not* making any more passes at me, that's where.'

'I'd be demolished,' he said. 'But I'm pretty sure it isn't all one-sided.'

Another deadly little silence enveloped the balcony.

Holly opened her mouth but had to close it as no inspiration came to her. In all honesty, how could she deny the claim? On the other hand, every bit of good sense she possessed told her that to acknowledge it would be foolhardy in the extreme.

So, in the end, she did the only thing available to her: she swung on her heel and walked away from him.

'How was the ball?' Mike Rafferty enquired of his boss the next morning.

Brett lay back in his chair and appeared to meditate for a moment. 'Interesting,' he said at last.

'Well, that's got to be better than you expected,' Mike

replied and placed some papers on the desk. 'The lead up to the wedding,' he said simply.

Brett grimaced and pulled the details of Mark's pre-wedding festivities towards him. 'I just hope it's not a three-ring circus. Oh hell, another ball!'

'But this one's just a normal ball,' Mike pointed out.

Brett did not look mollified as he read on. 'A soirée, a beach barbecue, a trip to the reef—da-da, da-da.' Brett waved a hand. 'All right. I presume they've got someone in to organize it all properly?'

Mike hesitated and then coughed nervously.

Brett stared narrowly at him. 'Who? Not...? Not Natasha?'

'I'm afraid so.'

Brett swore.

'She is the best—at this kind of thing,' Mike offered.

'But I believe they had someone else to start with who made a real hash of things, so they called on Ms Hewson and she saved the day, apparently. She and Aria are friends,' he added.

'I see.' Brett drummed his fingers on the desk then looked to have made a decision. 'Mike, find out all you can about a girl called Holly Harding. She's Richard Harding's daughter—the well-known writer—and I believe she's a journalist herself. Do it now, please.'

Mike stared at his boss for a moment as he tried to tie this in with Mark Wyndham's wedding.

'What?' Brett queried.

'Nothing,' Mike said hastily. 'Just going.'

* * *

On Monday afternoon Glenn Shepherd called Holly into his office, and hugged her. 'You're such a clever girl,' he enthused. 'I might have known I was laying down the gauntlet to you when I mentioned his name, but how on earth did you pull it off? And why keep it such a secret?' He released her and went back behind his desk.

Holly, looking dazed and confused, sank into a chair across the desk. 'What are you talking about, Glenn?'

'Getting an interview with Brett Wyndham, of course. What else?'

Holly stared at him, transfixed, then she cleared her throat. 'I—wasn't aware that I had.'

Glenn gestured. 'Well, there are a few details he wants to sort out with you before he gives his final consent, so I made an appointment for you with him for five-thirty this afternoon.' He passed a slip of paper to her over the desk. 'If you've got anything on, cancel it. This could be your big break, Holly, and it won't do *us* any harm, either. Uh—there may be some travel involved.'

'Travel?'

'I'll let him tell you about it but of course we'd foot the bill where necessary.'

'Glenn…' Holly said.

But he interrupted her and stood up. 'Go get it, girl! And now I've got to run.'

At five-twenty that afternoon, Holly glanced at the piece of paper Glenn had given her and frowned. Southbank was a lovely precinct on the Brisbane river, opposite the tall towers of the CBD. It was made up of restaurants, a swimming lagoon and gardens set around the civic theatre and the art gallery. It was not exactly where she would have expected to conduct a business meeting with Brett Wyndham.

Then again, that was the last thing she'd expected to be doing this Monday afternoon, or any afternoon, so why quibble at the venue?

She parked her car, gathered her tote bag and for a moment wished she was dressed more formally. But that would have involved rushing home to change, and anyway, she didn't want him to think she'd gone to any trouble with her appearance on his behalf, did she?

No, she answered herself, *so why even think it*?

Because she might have felt more mature, or something like that, if she wasn't dressed as she usually was for work.

She looked down at her jeans, the pink singlet top she wore under a rather beloved jacket and her brown, short boots. This was the kind of clothes she felt comfortable in when she was traveling, as well as at work.

As for her hair, she'd left it to its own devices that morning and the result was a mass of untamed curls.

There could be little or no resemblance to the girl at the shelter lunch or Holly Golightly, she reasoned, which should be a good thing.

But, she also reasoned, really her clothes and hair were nothing compared to her absolute shock and disbelief at this move Brett Wyndham had made. What was behind it?

She shook her head, locked her car and went to find him.

It took a moment for Brett Wyndham to recognize Holly Harding. He noticed a tall girl in denims and a pink singlet with a leather tote hanging from her shoulder, wandering down the path from the car park. He noted that she looked completely natural, with no make-up, from her wild, fair curls to her boots, as well as looking young and leggy. Then it suddenly dawned on him who she was.

He saw her look around the restaurant terrace—their designated meeting place—and he raised a hand. He thought she hesitated briefly, then she came over.

He stood up and offered her a chair. 'Good day,' he murmured as they both sat down. 'Yet another incarnation of Holly Harding?'

'This is the real me,' Holly said dryly, and studied him briefly. He wore a black sweater, olive-canvas trousers and thick-soled black-leather shoes. His short, dark hair was ruffled; while he might have made a perfect Spanish aristocrat a few nights ago, today he looked tough, inscrutable and potentially dangerous.

'Would you like a drink?'

'Just a soft one, thank you. I never mix business with pleasure,' Holly replied.

He ordered a fruit juice for her and beer for himself, ignoring her rather pointed comment. 'If this is the real you,' he said, 'What makes you moonlight as a social butterfly?'

'My mother. Please don't make any smart remarks,' she warned, and explained the situation to him in a nutshell.

'Very commendable.' He paused as his beer was served, along with a silver dish of olives and a fruit-laden glass of juice topped by a pink parasol for Holly.

'But a bit trying at times,' Holly revealed, allowing

her hostilities to lapse for a moment. 'I think I would have preferred standing on a street corner with a collection box rather than that lunch, but perhaps I shouldn't say that in deference to your sister.' She eyed him curiously then stared out over the gardens towards the river. The sun was setting and the quality of light was warm and vivid.

He watched her thoughtfully. 'Each to his own method, but we seem to have a few things in common.'

'Not really,' Holly disagreed, going back to clearly hostile, and turned to look straight at him. 'Why have you done this?'

He countered with a question, 'Did you or did you not tell your mother you would love to interview me?'

'I...' Holly paused. 'I told her an interview with you could provide the boost my career needed. I told her that I'd had no idea who you were, but if there'd ever been any chance of an interview I'd blown it.'

'Only, being a mother, she didn't believe you,' he said wryly. 'Well, it *is* on, on certain conditions.'

'So I hear.' She glanced at him coolly, as if she was highly suspicious of his conditions—which she was. 'What are they?'

'I'm a bit pressed for time. I need to be in Cairns—Palm Cove, precisely. I have an important meeting. And I need to be out at Haywire the following day for a few days. It's the only free time I have before my brother gets married, and anyway—' he looked at her over the rim of his glass '—it will set the scene for you.'

'You—want me to come to Palm Cove and then on to this Haywire place with you?' she queried a little jaggedly.

He nodded. 'Not only am I pressed for time, but logistically it makes sense. The best way to get you to Haywire is for you to fly out there with me from Cairns.'

'Do I,' Holly gestured, 'actually have to see this Haywire place?'

'Yes.'

'Why?'

He sat back and shoved his hands into his pockets with a slight frown. 'That doesn't sound like a dedicated journalist. Why wouldn't you want to see it?'

'Mr Wyndham,' she said carefully, 'You have not only accused me of being a serial socialite and a gold-digger, you've mentally undressed me often enough to make me *seriously* wary of being stuck somewhere out beyond the black stump with you!'

Like lightning, a crooked grin creased his face which didn't impress Holly at all.

'I apologize,' he said then. 'I was—' he paused to consider '—not in a very good mood—not at the lunch, anyway. However, you'd be quite safe at Haywire. There's staff up there, and I'm not in the habit of forcing myself on unwilling women.'

Holly chewed her lip then said finally, 'What are the other conditions?'

'I mainly want to talk about the work I do—so nothing personal, unless it's ancient history. And I want to vet it before it gets published.'

Holly blinked several times, then she said frustratedly, 'Why me?'

He shrugged. 'Why not? Not only are you a journalist, but you're interesting.' He looked amused. 'I've never been walked-out on before, as you did at the lunch. I've never been told I was making a pass in a French accent. And I've *never* been accused of being as bad-minded as a leopard.'

Holly realized she'd been staring at him open-mouthed. She shut it hastily and watched him twirl his beer bottle in his long fingers before pouring the last of it into his glass.

'But what really decided me,' he continued, 'was your mother.'

'My mother?' Holly repeated in dazed tones. 'How come?'

'I thought what she did was quite brave. Maybe it's mistaken maternal faith—we'll see, I guess—but I liked her for it.'

Holly was seized by strong emotion and had to turn away to hide it as her eyes blazed. If it killed her, she would dearly love to prove to Brett Wyndham that her mother's faith in her was not *mistakenly maternal*, even if it meant spending some days with him at Palm Cove and beyond the black stump...

After all, there was bound to be staff at the station, and Palm Cove was highly civilized, wasn't it? It was not as if she'd be stranded in some jungle with him. It would actually be quite difficult to be stalked by him up there, as predator and prey, and she was no silly girl to be seduced by palm trees and mango daiquiris.

Was that all there was to it, however? Was simply to be in his company seductive? Was he just that kind of man? She couldn't deny he'd had a powerful effect on her a couple of times—without even trying too hard, she thought a little bitterly. But surely that was in *her* power to control? Well, if not control, ignore.

After all, was she not getting gold in return for a little self-discipline?

She opened her mouth, looked frustrated and said, 'You never give interviews. So I'm having a little difficulty with that.'

'I'm branching out in a new direction that I was going to publicize anyway. I've read some of your pieces, you have your father's touch and I thought you could do justice to it.'

Holly's lips parted and he could see the quickening of interest drowning the doubt and suspicion in her eyes. 'Am I allowed to know what it is?'

He shook his head. 'Not yet. But it's the very good reason for you to see Haywire.'

Holly looked unamused. 'I find you extremely— annoying at times,' she told him.

Brett Wyndham's lips twisted; he wondered what she'd say if he told her how annoyed he'd been when they'd first met. He'd been annoyed at the lunch; he'd arrived annoyed, then got further annoyed at finding himself feeling a niggle of attraction towards the kind of girl he'd castigated to himself so thoroughly. When she'd walked out, the niggle had become tinged with a grudging kind of admiration—that had also annoyed him.

Then her Holly Golightly hauteur had claimed his attention, and on discovering it was the same girl his annoyance had turned to intrigue. He was still intrigued by this version of Holly Harding—even more intrigued because he was quite sure he'd stirred some response in her...

Still, he reflected, these were improbable lengths to go to over a smattering of intrigue to do with a woman, particularly for him. But he had liked her fresh, slightly zany style in the pieces he'd read, he reminded himself, and he had even considered the possibility of offering her some publicity work for his new venture.

'So?' He lifted an eyebrow at her.

Holly meditated for a moment then replied quite candidly. 'I'd love to say no, because you've pressed a few wrong buttons with me, Mr Wyndham. But—' she flipped her hand '—you've also pressed a few right ones. My mother was an inspired one, in more ways than one.' She cast him a strange little look from beneath her lashes. 'Then there's my editor. How I would explain to him I've knocked back this opportunity, I can't even begin to think.'

She paused to take several breaths.

'There's more?' he queried with some irony.

'A bit more. You've got to be interesting—you've certainly captured the public's imagination—so, on a purely professional level, I can't turn it down.'

'Am I expected to be flattered?'

Holly searched his eyes and could just detect the wicked amusement in their dark depths. 'Yes,' she said baldly. 'I'm usually no pushover.'

'OK, take it as read that I'm flattered.' He stopped, flagged a passing waiter and ordered a bottle of champagne.

'Oh. No!' Holly protested. 'I didn't mean...'

'You don't think we should celebrate?' He looked

offended. 'I do. It's not every day I score a coup like this. Besides, I thought you liked champagne.'

'You're making fun of me,' she accused.

'Yes,' he agreed. 'Well, yes and no. You can be quite an impressive twenty-four-year-old. Thanks,' he said to the waiter who delivered the champagne and carefully poured two glasses.

He handed one to Holly and held up his own. 'Cheers!'

Holly reluctantly raised her glass to his. 'Cheers,' she echoed. 'But I'm only having one glass. On top of everything else, I'm driving.'

'That's fine,' he said idly.

'Isn't that a waste of champagne? Or are you going to drink it all?'

'No. I'm meeting someone else here shortly. She also likes champagne.'

Holly took a hurried gulp. 'Well, the sooner I get going the better.'

'No need to rush; she's my sister.'

Holly looked embarrassed. 'Oh. I thought...' She tailed off.

'You thought she was a girlfriend?'

'Yes. Sorry. Not that it matters to me one way or the other.'

'Naturally not,' he murmured.

She eyed him over her glass. 'You know, I can't quite make you out.'

He allowed his dark gaze to drift over her in a way that caused her skin to shiver of its own accord. She'd been inwardly congratulating herself on *not* having this happen to her during this encounter—an involuntary physical response to this man—but now it had.

'The same goes for me,' he said quietly. 'Can't quite make you out.'

Holly made an effort to rescue herself, to stop the flow of messages bombarding her senses. How could it happen like this? she wondered a little wildly. Out of the blue across a little glass-topped table on a terrace in the fading light of day.

But her rather tortured reflections were broken by a canine yelp, a squeal then howls of pain as, limping badly, a dog skittered across the terrace and disappeared into the shrubbery.

CHAPTER THREE

HOLLY jumped to her feet but Brett Wyndham was even quicker.

He plunged into the shrubbery, issuing a terse warning to her over his shoulder to be careful because the dog, in its pain, could bite.

The next few minutes were chaotic as Brett captured then subdued the terrified dog, a black-and-white border collie. How, Holly had no idea, but he did, and a lot of people milled around. None of them was its owner, or had any idea where it had come from, other than it must have got loose from somewhere and possibly got run over as it had crossed the road.

'OK.' Brett pulled his phone out and tossed it to Holly. 'Find the nearest vet surgery.' He pulled out his car keys and tossed them to her. 'And drive my car down here as close as you can get. It's the silver BMW.'

Holly grabbed her tote and did so, and ended up driving the four-wheel-drive so Brett could attend to the dog on the way to the surgery. He was staunching a deep cut on its leg with his handkerchief and she heard him say, 'You're going to be all right, mate.'

She found the surgery with the aid of the GPS and

helped carry the dog in. 'Is he really going to be all right?' she asked fearfully as they handed it over.

'I reckon so.' He scanned her briefly then looked more closely. 'You better sit down; you look a bit pale. I'm going in for a few minutes.' He turned to the receptionist, who was hovering. 'Could you get her a glass of water?'

'Of course. Sit down, ma'am.'

Holly was only too glad to do so. A mobile phone with an unfamiliar ring sounded in her tote. She blinked, remembered it must be Brett's phone and after a moment's hesitation answered it.

'Brett Wyndham's phone.'

'Where is he and who are you?' an irate female voice said down the line.

Holly explained and added, 'Can I give him a message?'

'Oh.' The voice sounded mollified. 'Yes, if you wouldn't mind. It's his sister, Sue. I'm waiting for him at Southbank, but I'm going out to dinner so I won't wait any longer. Could you tell him I'll catch up with him tomorrow?'

Ten minutes later Brett reappeared and held his hand out to Holly. 'Let's go. He's got a broken leg, as well as the cut, but he'll be fine. He's in good hands, and he's got a microchip so they'll be able to track down his owner.'

'Thank heavens.' She got to her feet.

'How are you?' he queried.

'OK.'

He studied her narrowly. 'You don't altogether look it.'

'I...I once lost a dog in an accident. He was also a border collie. I called him Oliver, because as a puppy he was always looking for more food. He was run over, but he died. It just took me back a bit.'

Brett released her hand and put an arm around her shoulder. He didn't say anything, but Holly discovered herself to be comforted. Comforted and then something else—acutely conscious of Brett Wyndham.

She breathed in his essence—pure man—and she felt the long, strong lines of his body. She was reminded of how quick and light on his feet he'd been, how he'd used the power of his personality and expertise to calm the dog—but above all how he'd impressed her on a mental level, and now on a physical one.

'Better?' he queried.

'Yes, thanks.'

They stepped out onto the pavement, but he stopped. It was almost dark. 'My sister,' he said with a grimace and reached for his phone, but it wasn't there.

Holly retrieved it from her bag and gave him the message.

'OK.' He steered her towards his car.

'If you drop me off at the parking lot...' Holly began.

He shook his head. 'You still look as if you could do with a drink.'

'No. Thanks, but no. Anyway, we left the restaurant without paying!'

He shrugged and opened the car door. 'They know me. In you get—and don't argue, Holly Golightly.'

Holly had no choice but to do as she was told, although she did say, '*My* car?'

'Mike will collect it.' He fired the engine.

'Who's Mike?'

'The miracle worker in my life.' He swung out into the traffic. 'The PA *par excellence*.'

Not much later, Holly was sitting on a mocha-colored leather settee in what was obviously a den. The walls were *café au lait*, priceless-looking scatter rugs dotted the parquet floor and wooden louvres framed the view of a dark sky but a tinsel-town view of the city lights.

Brett had poured her a brandy then she'd washed her face and hands and handed her car keys over to his PA. Brett had gone to take a shower.

She'd only taken a couple of sips but she was thinking deeply when he strolled back into the room. He'd changed into jeans and a shirt; his hair was towelled dry and spiky.

'Will you stay for dinner?' he queried as he poured his own brandy.

'No thank you,' Holly said automatically. 'You know, it's just struck me—this could look strange.'

'What could?' He sat down opposite her.

'Me flitting around with you.'

'In what respect?'

She glanced at him then looked away a little awkwardly. 'People might wonder if I've joined the long list of, well, perhaps not beautiful—I mean *they* were all probably stunning—but the long list of women you've squired around.'

'What long list is that?' he enquired in a deadpan kind of way that alerted her to the fact he was secretly laughing at her.

Holly went slightly pink but said airily, 'Just something I read somewhere. But, believe me, I have no ambition to do that. Unless...' she stopped, struck by a thought, and relaxed a bit. 'I'm not stunning enough or upmarket-looking enough to qualify? Don't answer that,' she said with a lightning smile. 'I'm just thinking aloud.' She sobered and contemplated her drink with a frown.

Does she have no idea of how unusually attractive she is? Brett Wyndham found himself wondering. *Maybe not*, he conceded. She certainly didn't appear to expect him to counter her claim that she wasn't stunning enough to qualify as someone he would "squire around".

On the other hand, she'd had to fight off a bandit and a sheikh, if she was to be believed, so...

He shrugged. 'I never bother with what people think.'

'You may be in a position not to bother—your reputation is already set,' she retorted. 'Mine is not.' Then she took a very deep breath. 'Please tell me why you're doing this.'

He rolled his glass in his hands then looked directly into her eyes. 'I'm intrigued. I can't believe you're not.' He paused. 'And I guess that's brought out the hunter instinct in me. At the same time, I *don't* ever force myself on unwilling women, if that's what's worrying you.'

Holly looked away. She paused and pressed her palms together tightly. 'And if I told you I don't have any interest in... Well, the thing is, I got my fingers pretty badly burnt once due to "chemistry". It's—it hasn't left me yet. I don't know if it ever will.'

He narrowed his eyes. 'Not the bandit or the sheikh, I gather?'

Holly waved her hand. 'Oh, no,' she said dismissively.

'I think you better tell me.'

She glanced at him from under her lashes, then smiled briefly. 'I don't think I should. It's supposed to be the other way round—you telling me stuff. And *you* have no intention of going into your private life.' She looked at him with some irony.

A silence lingered between them.

'So, should we just leave it there?' she suggested at last.

He stared at her pensively. 'Don't you want the interview now?'

'I thought you might have changed your mind.'

His lips twisted. 'Because I got my wrist slapped metaphorically? No, I haven't changed my mind.'

'But you won't—I mean—bring this up again?' she queried, her eyes dark and serious.

'Tell you what,' he drawled. '*I* won't say a word on the subject.'

Holly frowned. 'That sounds as if there's a trap there somewhere.'

'Sorry, it's the best I can come up with. So, are we on or off?'

She hesitated then put down her glass, stood up and walked over to the louvres that framed the city view. She was in two minds, she realized. She sensed an element of danger between her and Brett Wyndham, but she had to admit he'd been honest, whereas she hadn't—not entirely, anyway.

On the other hand, her career was vitally important to her. It had been her mainstay through some dark days.

She turned back to him. 'On. My journalistic instincts seem to have won the day,' she said ruefully. 'Can I go home now?'

'Of course.' He stood up, called for Mike Rafferty, and when he came asked him if he'd found Holly's car.

'Sure did,' Mike replied, and handed Holly the keys. 'It's parked downstairs, Miss Harding.'

'Thank you,' She hesitated then turned back to Brett Wyndham. 'Well, goodnight.'

'Goodnight, Holly,' he said casually, and turned away.

After he'd dined alone, Brett took his coffee to his study, where he intended to work on his next trip to Africa, only to find himself unable to concentrate.

The fact that it was a girl coming between him and his plans was unusual.

He swirled his coffee and lay back in his chair, Well, a change of direction in his life was on the cards; whilst he knew it was one he needed to make, would he ever be able to resist the call of the wild? Was that why he was unsettled?

It was a juggling act holding the reins of all the Wyndham enterprises based here and being away so frequently. Also, there was something niggling at him that he couldn't quite put his finger on, but he suspected it was the need to establish some roots.

In the meantime—in the short term, more accurately—a girl had come to his attention. A girl he wasn't at all sure about.

A girl who continued to hold him at arm's length, now with the claim that she'd had her fingers burnt due to "chemistry". How true was that? he wondered.

Could it all be part of a plan to hold his interest? He'd come across many a plan to hold his interest, he reflected dryly.

None of that changed the fact that she was attractive in a different kind of way—when did it ever? Good skin, beautiful eyes, clean, very slim lines; at times, sparkling intelligence and a cutting way with her repartee…

He smiled suddenly as he thought of her 'Holly Golightly from Tahiti' act.

He finished his coffee and contemplated another possibility. It was so long since any woman had said no to him he couldn't help but be intrigued. Especially as he could have sworn there'd been that edgy, sensual pull between them almost from the moment they'd first crossed swords.

Why, though, he wondered, had he gone to the lengths of dangling an interview before her?

Because she was likeable, kissable, different?

He drummed his fingers on the desk suddenly; or did he have in mind using her to deflect his ex-fiancée?

'I'm off to Cairns—well, Palm Cove—then the bush for a few days tomorrow,' Holly said to her mother that evening over a late dinner. She pushed away the remains of a tasty chicken casserole. 'You're not going to believe this, but I got the Brett Wyndham interview after all.'

Sylvia uttered a little cry of delight. 'Holly! That's

marvellous. I wasn't sure I did the right thing. I know you tried to gloss over it, but I wasn't sure whether you really approved.' Sylvia paused and frowned. 'But why do you have to go to Cairns?'

Holly made the swift decision to gloss over that bit and murmured something about Brett being short of time.

Sylvia mulled over this for a moment, then she said, 'He's very good-looking, isn't he? I mean he has a real presence, doesn't he?'

'I guess he does.'

'Holly,' Sylvia began, 'I know that awful thing that happened to you is not going to be easy to get over. Actually, you've been simply marvellous with the way—'

'Mum, don't,' Holly interrupted quietly.

'But there has to be the right man for you out there, darling,' Sylvia said passionately.

'There probably is, but it's not Brett Wyndham.'

'How can you be so sure?'

Holly moved the salt cellar to a different spot and sighed. 'It's just a feeling I have, Mum. For one thing, he's a billionaire, so he could have anyone and there's nothing so special about me. And, for me, I suppose it started with the way he behaved that day of the lunch. Then I read that he'd broken off his engagement to a girl who would have thought she was the last in a *long* line of women he'd escorted. And it seems,' she said bitterly, 'He's a master at getting his own way.'

'In view of all that,' Sylvia replied a shade tartly, 'I'm surprised you're going to Palm Cove and the bush.'

Holly shrugged. 'I once made the decision I wouldn't

be a victim, and what really helped me was my career. I can't knock back this opportunity to further it.'

Glenn Shepherd said to Holly the next morning, 'So it's all set up?'

'Yes. But there's no personal side to it, Glenn, other than "ancient history"—I guess that means how he grew up—and he wants to have final say. It's his work he wants to talk about, and some new project.'

'Even that's a scoop. So, you're off to Palm Cove and points west?'

Holly nodded then looked questioningly at her editor. 'How did you know that? I mean, so soon?'

'His PA has just been on the phone. They offered to pay for your flights; I knocked that back, but they will provide accommodation in Palm Cove—they own the resort, after all.'

Holly grimaced. 'I'd rather stay in a mud hut.'

'Holly, is there anything you're not telling me?' Glenn stared at her interrogatively.

'What do you mean?'

'I don't know.'

'No,' Holly replied. *'No.'*

'Enjoy yourself, then.'

Cairns, in Far North Queensland, was always a pleasure to visit, Holly reflected as she landed on a commercial flight and took the courtesy bus out of town to Palm Cove. With its mountainous backdrop, its beaches, its lush flora, bougainvillea, hibiscus in many colours, yellow allamanda everywhere and its warm, humid air, you got a delightful sense of the tropics.

It was also a touristy place—it was a stepping-off point for all the marvels of the Great Barrier Reef—but it wasn't brash. It was relaxed, yet still retained its solid country-town air.

Palm Cove, half an hour's drive north of Cairns, was exclusive.

Lovely resorts lined the road opposite the beach and there was a cosmopolitan air with open-air cafés and marvellous old melaleucas, or paper-bark trees, growing out of the pavements. There were upmarket restaurants and boutiques that would have made her mother's mouth water. The beach itself was a delight. Lined with cotton-woods, casuarinas and palms, it curved around a bay and overlooked Double Island and a smaller island she didn't know the name of. On a hot, still, autumn day, the water looked placid and immensely inviting. Whilst summer in the region might be a trial, autumn and winter—if you could call them that in the far north—were lovely.

The resort owned by the Wyndhams was built on colonial lines. It was spacious and cool and was right on the beach.

Holly unpacked her luggage in a pleasant room. It didn't take her long; she was used to travelling light and had evolved a simple wardrobe that nevertheless saw her through most eventualities. She'd resisted her mother's attempts to add to it.

She was contemplating going for a walk when she got a phone message: Mr Wyndham presented his compliments to Ms Harding; he had some time free and would like to see her in his suite in half an hour.

Ms Harding hesitated for a moment then agreed.

As she put the phone down, she felt a little trill of

annoyance at this high-handed invitation but immediately took herself to task. This was business, wasn't it?

She had a quick shower and put on jeans and a cotton blouse. But the humidity played havoc with her hair, so she decided to clip it back in order to control it.

That was when she found a surprise in her bag. Her mother had been unable to let her come to Palm Cove without some maternal input: she'd tucked in a little box of jewellery. Amongst the necklaces and bangles was a pair of very long, dangly bead-and-gilt earrings.

Holly stared at them then put them on.

Not bad, she decided, and tied her hair back.

Finally, with her feet in ballet pumps and her tote bag on her shoulder, she went to find Brett Wyndham's suite.

It was on the top floor of the resort with sweeping views of Palm Cove. Although the sun was setting in the west behind the resort, the waters of the cove reflected the time of day in a spectrum of lovely colours, apricot, lavender and lilac.

It was a moment before she took her eyes off the panorama after a waiter admitted her and ushered her into the lounge. Then she turned to the man himself, and got a surprise.

No casual clothes this time. Today he wore a grey suit and a blue-and-white-striped shirt. Today he looked extremely formal as he talked into his mobile phone.

Merely talking? Holly wondered. Or in the process of delivering an extremely cutting dressing-down as he stood half-turned away from her and fired words rather like bullets into the phone? Then he cut the connection, threw the phone down on a sofa in disgust and turned to her with his dark eyes blazing.

Holly swallowed in sudden fright and took a step backwards. 'Uh—hi!' she said uncertainly. 'Sorry, I didn't mean to interrupt. Maybe I'll just go until your temper has cooled a bit.' She turned away hurriedly.

He reached her in two strides and spun her back with his hands on her shoulders. 'Don't think you can walk out on me, Holly Harding.'

Holly stared up at him, going rigid and quite pale with anger. 'Let me *go*!'

Brett Wyndham paused, frowned down at her then let his hands drop to his side. 'I'm sorry,' he said quietly and went over to a drinks trolley. 'Here.' He brought her back a brandy.

'I don't—'

'Holly...' he warned.

'All I ever seem to do is drink either champagne or brandy in your presence,' she said frustratedly.

A faint smile twisted his lips. 'Sit down,' he said, and when she hesitated he added 'Let me explain. In certain circumstances I have a very short fuse.'

'So it would appear,' she agreed wholeheartedly.

He pulled off his jacket. 'Yes, well.' He gestured towards the phone. 'That was news that a breeding pair of black rhino—highly endangered now in Africa—has been injured in transit. I bought them from a zoo where they were patently *not* breeding due to stress, too small a habitat and so on.'

'Oh,' Holly said and sank into a chair, her imagination captured—so much so, she forgot her fright of a few minutes ago. 'Badly injured? In a road accident or what? A road accident,' she answered herself. 'That's why you were informing the person on the other end of the phone—' she glanced over at his mobile phone lying on the sofa opposite '—that he must have got his driving licence out of a cornflake packet. Amongst everything else you said.'

Brett Wyndham grinned fleetingly. 'Yes. But no, not badly injured. All the same, their numbers are shrinking at such an alarming rate, it's a terrifying thought, losing even two. And it only adds to their stress.'

'I see.' She frowned. 'Not that I see where I come into it. Are you trying to tell me that when your short fuse explodes anyone within range is liable to cop it?'

'It's been known to happen,' he agreed. 'However, there was a grain of truth in what I said. By the way, your hair looks nice. But I have an aversion to long, dangly earrings.'

Holly raised her eyebrows. 'Why?'

He said, 'A girl invited me home for dinner once. I arrived on time with a bunch of flowers and a bottle of wine. She opened the door. She had her hair all pulled back and all she wore were long dangly earrings, high heels and a G-string.'

Holly gasped.

'Exactly how I reacted,' he said gravely. 'Only I dropped the flowers as well.'

'What did you do then?' Holly was now laughing helplessly.

'I was younger,' he said reflectively. 'What did I do? I suggested to her that maybe she was putting the cart before the horse.'

'Oh no! What did she do?'

'She said that if all she'd achieved was to bring to mind a cart horse—not what I'd meant at all—she was wasting her time, and she slammed the door in my face. Of course, I've often wondered whether it didn't fall more into a "looking a gift horse in the mouth" scenario or "horses for courses".'

'Don't go on!' Holly held a hand to her side. 'You're making me laugh too much.'

'The worst part about it is I often find myself undressing women with long, dangly earrings to this day—only mentally, of course.'

'Oh, no!' Holly was still laughing as she removed her earrings. 'There. Am I safe?'

He took his tie off and unbuttoned his collar as he studied her—rather acutely—and nodded. 'Yes.' He paused and seemed to change his mind about something. 'OK. Shall we begin?'

Holly felt her heart jolt. 'The interview?'

'What else?' he queried a little dryly.

'Nothing! I mean, um, I didn't realize you wanted to start tonight—but I've made some notes that I brought with me,' she hastened to assure him and reached for her bag.

He sat down. 'Where do you want to start?'

She drew a notebook from her tote and a pen. She nibbled the end of the pen for a moment and a subtle change came over her.

She looked at Brett Wyndham meditatively, as if sizing him up, then said, 'Would you like to give me a brief background-history of the family? I have researched it, but you would have a much more personal view, and you may be able to pinpoint where the seeds of this passion you have for saving endangered-species came from.'

'Animals always fascinated me,' he said slowly. 'And growing up on a station gave me plenty of experience with domestic ones, as well as the more exotic wild ones—echidnas, wombats and so on. I also remember my grandmother; she was renowned as a bush vet, although she wasn't qualified as one. But she always had—' he paused to grin '—a houseful of baby wallabies she'd rescued, or so it seemed to me anyway. She used to hang them up in pillow slips as if they were still in their mother's pouch.'

'So how far back does the Wyndham association with Far North Queensland go...?'

An hour later, Brett glanced at his watch and Holly took the hint. She put her pen and notebook back into her tote, but she was satisfied with their progress. Brett had given her an insight into how the Wyndham fortune had been built, as well as a fascinating insight into life on cattle stations in the Cape York area in the early part of the twentieth century—gleaned, he told her, from his grandmother's stories and diaries. And he'd included a few immediate-family anecdotes.

'Thank you,' she said warmly. 'That was a really good beginning. It's always important to be able to set the scene.' She drained her brandy. 'And I'll try not to require any more medicinal brandy for our next session.'

He stood up and reached for his jacket. 'I'm sorry; I have a dinner to attend, but you're welcome to use the resort dining-room on us.'

Holly slung her bag on her shoulder. 'Oh no, but thank you. I was planning to wander down the waterfront and indulge in a thoroughly decadent hamburger at one of the cafés, then an early night. We are still flying to Haywire early tomorrow, I take it?'

'Yes. I plan to leave here at nine sharp. I'll pick you up at Reception.' He hesitated and frowned.

Holly studied him. 'Are you having second thoughts?' she queried.

'No. But you're good,' he said slowly. 'Especially for one so young.'

'Good?' She looked puzzled.

'You seem to have the art of putting a person at ease down to a fine art.'

'Thank you,' Holly murmured. 'Why do I get the feeling you don't altogether approve, though?' she added.

'Could you be imagining it?' he suggested with a sudden grin, and went on immediately, 'I am running late now; I'm sorry...'

'Going; I'm going!' Holly assured him and turned towards the door. 'See you tomorrow.'

But, even though he *was* running late, Brett Wyndham watched her retreating back until she disappeared. Then he walked out on to the terrace and stared at the moon and the river of silver light it was pouring onto the waters of the cove.

She'd been right, he reflected. He wasn't entirely approving of her skills as an interviewer. She did have an engaging, relaxing way with her. She did also have an undoubted enthusiasm for, and a lively curiosity about, his story and that of his family and its history. Not that he'd told her anything he hadn't wanted to tell her, nor did he have any intention of exposing the dark secret that lay behind him.

But was she capable of digging it out somehow?

Or, in other words, had he unwittingly put himself into a rather vulnerable situation because he'd under-estimated a leggy twenty-four-year old who intrigued him?

For some reason his thoughts moved on to the little scene that had played out when she'd first arrived in his suite, and how she'd reacted when he'd stopped her walking out. She'd been genuinely frightened and angry at the same time. She *had* told him she'd got her fingers burnt once and it was still with her. He had to believe that now. He also had to believe it had pulled him up short, the fact that he'd frightened her.

All the same—call it all off and send her home? Or deliberately shift the focus to the project he really wanted to publicize, as had been his original intention?

He shrugged and went out to dinner with his brother, his sister, his sister-in-law-to-be and several others. He was unaware that his ex-fiancée would be one of the party.

Holly had her hamburger, and was strolling along the beach side of the road opposite the fabulous restaurants of Palm Cove, when she stopped as Brett Wyndham caught her attention.

He was with a party of diners at an upmarket restau-rant that opened onto the pavement and had an amazing old melaleuca tree growing in the middle of it. It was not only an upmarket restaurant, it was a pretty upmarket party of diners, she decided. One of the women was his sister, Sue Murray, looking lovely in turquoise silk with pearls in her ears and around her neck. Two of the other women were exceptionally sleek and gorgeously dressed, one a stunning redhead, the other with a river of smooth, straight blonde hair that Holly would have given her eye teeth for.

It looked to be a lively party as wine glasses glinted beneath the lights and a small army of waiters delivered a course.

After her initial summing-up of the party, Holly turned her attention back to Brett and felt that not so unexpected frisson run through her. She frowned. Was she getting used to the effect his dark good looks and tall physique had on her? She certainly wasn't as annoyed about it as she'd been only a few days ago.

But there was something else to worry about now, she acknowledged. Ever since she'd left his suite she'd been conscious of a sense of unease. *Was* she imagining it, or had he rather suddenly developed reservations about the interview?

No, it wasn't her imagination, she decided. Something had changed. Had she asked too many questions?

She shook her head and went back to watching Brett Wyndham, only to be troubled by yet another set of thoughts. How would she feel if he pulled out of the interview? How would she feel if she never saw him again?

Her eyes widened at the chill little pang that ran through her at the thought, leaving her in no doubt she would suffer a sense of loss, a sense of regret. If that was the case for her now, after only a few brief encounters, how dangerous could it be to get to know Brett Wyndham better?

CHAPTER FOUR

HOLLY decided to go for a swim as dawn broke over Palm Cove the next morning.

She put on her swimsuit, a pretty peasant blouse and a skimpy pair of shorts. She laid out the clothes she would wear after her swim and looked at her luggage, all neatly packed. The only thing that wasn't quite neat and tidy in her mind was, which way would she go when she left Palm Cove? Out to Haywire, or back to Brisbane?

She collected a towel from the pool area and walked through the quiet resort to the beach.

There was a sprinkling of early-morning walkers and swimmers and, even so early, a feel of the coming heat of the day on the air.

She hesitated then opted to go for a walk first.

Palm Cove—most of Far North Queensland, for that matter—didn't offer blinding white sand on its beaches, although its off-shore islands might. What you got instead was sand that resembled raw sugar but it was clean, and towards the waterline, firm.

What also impressed her was that from further down the beach you would not have known Palm Cove was there, thanks to the height limitations put on the buildings and the trees that lined the beach.

She strode out and reviewed her dilemma as she did so. If she did go back to Brisbane off her own bat—assuming she wasn't sent back, and she had the feeling it wasn't impossible for that to be on the cards—how would she handle it? She would have to confess to Glenn and her mother that she'd been unable to handle the Wyndham interview, and she would go back to travel reporting with a sense of relief.

If she did get sent back, though, she'd have to confess that she must have pressed some wrong buttons with Brett Wyndham.

In either case, she would not even contemplate the fact that at times Brett Wyndham fascinated her mentally and stirred her physically, probably more than any man had done. Well, she could tell herself that, anyway.

It would be true to say she was still on the horns of a dilemma when she got back to her towel. She shrugged frustratedly, dropped her top and shorts on it and waded into the water. It was heavenly, refreshing but not cold, calm, buoyant; when it was up to her knees, she dived in and swam out energetically.

After about ten minutes, she swam back to where she could stand and floated on her back, feeling rejuvenated—cleansed, even—as if she'd experienced a catharsis and could put the whole sorry business behind her one way or another.

'Morning, Holly.'

She sank, swallowed some water and came up spluttering. Brett Wyndham, with his dark hair plastered to his head, was standing a few feet away from her, his tanned shoulders smooth and wet.

'What are you doing here?' she demanded, somewhat indistinctly, through a fit of coughing.

He looked around. 'I thought it was a public beach.'

'Of course it is!' She felt for the bottom with her toes. 'I mean—it doesn't matter.'

'Have I done something to annoy you?' he queried gravely.

Holly lay back in the water and rippled it with her fingers. Then she sat up and flicked her gaze from the strong brown column of his throat, from his sleek outline, and eyed a line of opal-pale clouds above, then their reflection on the glassy surface of the sea. 'I thought it might be the other way round.'

He raised an eyebrow. 'Why?'

'I thought—I thought you were having second thoughts last night.'

She moved a few steps towards the beach, then something swirled in the water next to her; she jerked away and fell over with a cry of fright.

'Holly!' Brett plunged to her side and lifted her into his arms. 'What was it? Are you hurt?'

'I don't know what it was. I don't think I'm hurt, though. I just got a fright!'

'OK.' He carried her up the beach and put her down on her towel. 'Let's have a look.'

He could find no wound on her feet or legs and he looked patently relieved.

Holly sat up. 'What could it have been?'

'It could have been a stingray.'

She stared at him round-eyed. 'That could have been fatal!'

He smiled. 'Not necessarily, not in your feet and legs, but it can take a long time to heal.'

Holly allowed a long breath to escape. 'So, a serpent in paradise, you could say.'

'Mmm… Have you had breakfast?'

'No. Uh, no, but—'

'Come and have it with me.' He stood up.

Holly stared up at him. He wore a colourful pair of board shorts; as she'd always suspected, his physique was outstanding: not an ounce of excess weight and whipcord muscles. There was only one way to describe it: he was beautifully proportioned. Tall, lean, strong as well as dark, and pirate-like—altogether enough to set her pulses fluttering.

She swallowed and realized she was on the receiving end of his scrutiny. His dark gaze lingered on her legs, her waist and the curve of her breasts beneath the fine lycra of her costume, as well as the pulse beating at the base of her throat. She found herself feeling hot and cold as her nipples peaked visibly.

She jumped up. 'Thanks, but no thanks. I really…' She picked up her towel and flapped it vigorously. 'I really got the feeling last night that things had gone sour somehow, and it might be best if I just go back to Brisbane, so—'

'Holly.' He wrested the towel from her. 'Before you cover us completely with sand, if you still want to go after breakfast, fine. But I haven't told you about my new project yet—my plans to open a zoo.'

Holly went still and blinked at him. 'A zoo?' she repeated.

'Yes, I'm planning one along the lines of the Western

Plains zoo outside Dubbo, but up here on Haywire—
that's why I wanted you to see it. I'm thinking of an
adopt-an-animal scheme as a means of publicizing it,
as well as the whole endangered-species issue.'

Her eyes widened. 'What a great idea! Tell me
more.'

He shook his head. 'You have to come to breakfast
if you want any more details.'

She clicked her tongue. 'You're extremely domineer-
ing, aren't you?'

He shrugged and handed her back her towel.

He ordered breakfast to be served on the terrace of his
suite.

Holly sat outside waiting for it while he made and
received some phone calls to do with the welfare of his
rhinos, and she tried to work out a plan of action.

Nothing had occurred to her by the time breakfast
arrived. It was a ceremonial delivery. There was champagne and orange juice; there was a gorgeous fruit-plat-
ter with some of the unusual fruits found in the area, like
rambutans and star-fruit; there was yoghurt and cereal,
a mushroom omelette for her and eggs and bacon for
him.

The toast was wrapped in a linen napkin and there
was a silver flask of coffee.

'Thank you, we'll help ourselves,' Brett murmured,
and the team of waiters withdrew discreetly.

'I'll never eat all this,' Holly said ruefully.

'Eat as much or as little as you like. I usually start
with the main course then work my way backwards,

with the fruit topped with a little yoghurt—as dessert, you might say.'

'Really?' Holly eyed him with some intrigue. 'That's a novel approach.'

'Try it.'

'I will. By the way, how long would we stay at Haywire, assuming we go?'

He glanced at her. 'Two or three days.'

'You did mention your brother's wedding.'

He glanced at his watch to check the date. 'That's a week from today, here.'

'Here?'

'Uh-huh, but there are a few preliminaries in the form of balls, soirées, a reef trip et cetera.'

Holly had to smile. 'You don't sound impressed.'

'I'm not.' He shrugged. 'But he is my brother. OK—the zoo.' He started on his eggs and bacon, and gave her the broad outline of his plans for the zoo—the size of the paddocks he intended to create, the animals he wanted and some of the difficulties involved.

'Impressive,' she said. 'I think it's a marvellous idea. But…' She pushed away her plate and picked up a prickly purple rambutan, wondering at the same time how you were supposed to eat it. 'But I'm not sure I'm the right person to do this. What I mean is, I'm not sure *you* think I am.' She watched him keenly for a long moment.

He reached for the coffee pot, poured two cups and pushed one towards her. 'I do think you're right for it. I think you have fresh, innovative views.'

'But something changed last night,' she persisted quietly.

He looked out over the water and was silent for a time. *Yes, Holly Golightly,* he thought with an inward grimace, *some things did change last night—one you're not even aware of—but it's the reason I'm* not *putting you on the next plane down south.*

He clenched his fist as he thought of the dinner last night. His sister-in-law-to-be had decided she might be able to mend some fences, so she'd produced Natasha Hewson at the dinner with the disclaimer that the wedding next weekend was going to be all Nat's work of art, and they'd be bound to run into each other anyway.

So I'm back in the bloody position, he thought, gritting his teeth, *of using you, Ms Harding, to deflect my ex-fiancée.* Not that he had any expectations that the two would ever meet, because he intended to whisk her off to Haywire as planned this morning before she went back to Brisbane. But as soon as Nat knew he was travelling with a girl—and he had no doubt she would know it!—she might get the message.

Not exactly admirable behaviour, he mused rather grimly, *but needs must when the devil drives.*

'It occurred to me last night,' he said, switching his gaze suddenly back to Holly, 'That I might be going into areas I don't really want to go into—not any further, anyway.'

Holly looked puzzled for a moment and she opened her mouth to say that it had all been pretty harmless, surely? But she changed her mind at the last moment. It was, of course, his prerogative, but it raised a question mark in her mind.

'Um…' She hesitated and put the rambutan down.

'That's up to you. I'm happy to go along with whatever you want to talk about.'

'So.' His lips twisted. 'Are we on again?'

Holly looked down and felt a strong pull towards taking the safe path—the one that would get her away from the dangerous elements of this man. From the undoubted attraction she felt towards him—her fascination with the mystique behind him. But at the same time her feeling was that Brett Wyndham could not be a long=term prospect for her.

She thought briefly of the dinner party she'd witnessed last night and it struck her that, while the man himself embodied the kind of life she found fascinating, there had to be a dimension to his life that occupied another stratum—one she did not belong to—that of ultra-glamorous, gorgeously groomed, sleek and glossy women. Last night they'd all looked like models or film stars.

Should that not make her feel safe with him, however? The fact that she patently didn't look like a model or a film star…?

She shrugged at last. 'On. Again.'

They exchanged a long, probing glance until finally he said, 'I see. We're still in the same boat.'

She looked perplexed. 'Boat?'

'We can't quite make each other out.' He smiled, but a shade dryly. 'All right. Are you ready to fly out shortly?'

Holly hesitated momentarily, then nodded. She went away to change and collect her things.

As she changed into her jeans, a sunshine-yellow singlet top, her denim jacket and her boots, she stared at her image in the mirror a couple of times and realized she looked and felt tense, and didn't know how to deal with it.

Here she was about to step out into the wide blue yonder with a man she hardly knew—a man she'd clashed with but at the same time felt attracted to—and her emotions were, accordingly, in a bit of a tangle.

How was she going to revert to Holly Harding, journalist, on a very important mission?

She was still preoccupied with this question as she drove down the Bruce Highway with Brett Wyndham, between sugar cane fields, towards the city of Cairns in its circle of hills and the airport.

Brett piloted his own plane, she discovered later, still not quite able to believe what was happening to her. The plane was a trim little six-seater with a W on the tail.

She was still pinching herself metaphorically as the nose of the plane rose and the speeding runway fell away. She was also trying to decide how to handle things between them. Common sense told her a matter-of-fact approach was the only way to go, but even that wasn't going to be easy.

She waited until they reached their cruising altitude then asked him how long the flight would be.

He told her briefly.

'Can you talk?'

'Of course,' he replied.

'Could you give me a run-down on the country we're flying over and our destination?'

He did so. They were flying west over the old mining towns of the Tablelands towards volcanic country famous for its lava tubes; then the great, grassy lands of the savannah/gulf country, as in the Gulf of Carpentaria, where their destination lay.

'Haywire?' she repeated with a grin. 'Where did it get its name?

He grimaced. 'No-one seems to know.'

Holly glanced across at him. He looked thoroughly professional in a khaki bush-shirt and jeans, with his headphones on and his beautiful hands checking instruments.

Professional and withdrawn from her, she contemplated as her gaze was drawn to her own hands clasped rather forlornly in her lap.

Who was she to quibble about 'professional and withdrawn' being the order of the day? It was what she'd almost stipulated, wasn't it? The only problem was she needed to get him to open up if she was going to get full value out of this trip. But—big but—there was a fine line between getting him to talk easily and naturally from a professional point of view and not finding herself loving his company at the same time.

She shook her head and realized he was watching her.

She coloured a little.

'Some internal debate?' he suggested.

'You could say so. Where are we now?' She looked out at the panorama of red sandy earth below them, with its sage-green vegetation, at the undulations and the space.

'About halfway between Georgetown and Croydon. If you follow the Savannah Way it takes you on to Normanton and Karumba, on the gulf. Over that way,' he pointed, 'is Forsayth and Cobbold Gorge; it's quite amazing. And those are the Newcastle Ranges to the east, and the sandstone escarpment to the west.'

'It's very remote,' she said in awe. 'And empty.'

'Remote,' he agreed. 'Hot as hell in summer, but with quite a history, not only of cattle but gold rushes and gem fields. Georgetown has a gem museum and Croydon has a recreation of the life and times of the gold rush there.'

'They look so small, though—Georgetown and Croydon,' she ventured.

He shrugged. 'They are now. Last count, Georgetown had under three-hundred residents, but it's the heart of a huge shire, and they're both on the road to Karumba and the gulf, renowned for its fishing. With the army of grey nomads out and about these days, they get a lot of passing traffic.'

Holly grinned. 'Grey nomads' was the term given to retired Australians who travelled the continent in caravans or camper vans or just with tents. It could almost be said it was the national retiree-pastime.

Half an hour later they started to lose altitude and Brett pointed out the Haywire homestead. All Holly could see was a huddle of roofs and a grassy airstrip between white-painted wooden fences in a sea of scrub.

Then he spoke into his VHF radio, and over some static a female voice said she'd walked the strip and it was in good order.

'Romeo, coming in,' he responded.

Ten minutes later they made a slightly bumpy landing and rolled to a stop adjacent to the huddle of roofs Holly had seen from the air.

A girl and a dog came through the gate in the airstrip fence to meet them.

'Holly,' Brett said, 'This is Sarah. And this—' he bent down to pat the red cattle-dog who accepted his ministrations with every sign of ecstasy '—is Bella.'

'Welcome to Haywire, Holly,' Sarah said in a very English accent.

Holly blinked in surprise, and Brett and Sarah exchanged grins. 'Sarah is backpacking her way around the world,' Brett said. 'How long have you been with us now?' he asked the English girl.

'Three months. I can't seem to tear myself away!' Sarah said ruefully. 'Brett, since you're here, I'm a bit worried about one of the mares in the holding paddock— she's lame. Would you mind having a look at her? I could show Holly around a bit in the meantime.'

'Sure. I'll leave you to it.'

Haywire homestead was a revelation to Holly in as much as it wasn't a homestead at all in the accepted sense of the word. All the accommodation was in separate cabins set out on green lawns and inside a fence designed to keep wallabies, emus and other wildlife out, according to Sarah.

All the other facilities were under one huge roof: lounge area, dining area, a small library-cum-games room et cetera. But the unique thing was, there were no outside walls.

The floor was slate; there was a central stone-fire-place, and at intervals there were tubs of potted plants and artistically arranged pieces of dead wood, often draped with ferns.

There was a long refectory table, comfortable cane-loungers and steamer chairs; beyond the fence and lawn, looking away from the rest of the compound, there was a lake alive with birds, reeds and water lilies.

The whole area reminded Holly of a safari lodge, and she was most impressed.

'Just one thing, what do you do when it rains or blows a gale?' she asked Sarah ruefully.

'Hasn't happened to me yet,' Sarah replied. 'But there are roll-down blinds.' She pointed them out. 'And I believe they put up shutters if they get a cyclone. Otherwise it lets the air flow through when it's really hot. Here's the kitchen.'

The kitchen was not visible from the rest of the area; it was also open on one side, yet had all mod cons. There were, Holly learnt, several sources of power on Haywire: a generator for electricity and gas for the hot-water system. There were still some old-fashioned combustion stoves for heating water in case other means failed. And there was a satellite phone as well as a VHF radio for communications.

There was an above-ground swimming pool surrounded by emerald lawn and shaded by trees.

Sarah explained that she was actually a nurse, but she enjoyed cooking, she loved the outback and she loved horses, so a stint as a housekeeper at Haywire suited her down to the ground.

'Mind you, most often there's only me, Bella, the horses and a few stockmen here. We don't get to see the family that often. Actually, I'm surprised to see Brett. I thought he'd be down at Palm Cove with the rest of them.'

'We were—he was,' Holly said, and intercepted a curious little glance from Sarah. She found herself thinking, *I knew this would happen! Probably no passable woman is safe in Brett Wyndham's company without being thought of as his lover.* 'I'm actually working with him,' she added.

'So she is,' the man in question agreed as he strolled up to them.

They both turned.

'The mare has a stone bruise in her off-fore. I've relieved the pressure, but keep an eye on her or get Kane to,' he added to Sarah. 'Are they coming in tonight? Kane,' he said for Holly's benefit, 'Is station foreman, and he has two offsiders.'

Sarah shook her head. 'They've got a problem with a fence on the northern boundary. That's miles away, so they decided to camp out overnight.'

'OK, then it's just us. I'm going to take Holly for a drive; we'll be back before dark. Incidentally, what's for dinner?'

Sarah grinned her infectious grin. 'Would you believe? Roast beef!'

'Standard cattle-station joke—roast beef for dinner,' Brett said to Holly as they climbed into a sturdy, high-chassis four-wheel-drive utility vehicle. Holly had brought her camera.

She laughed, but said, 'Look, I'm really surprised at how few people you have working here. From memory you run ten-thousand head of cattle; that sounds like a huge herd to me, and Haywire covers thousands of square kilometers.' Holly said.

'That's because you probably don't know much about Brahman and Droughtmaster cattle.'

'I know nothing,' Holly confessed.

'Well—' he swung the wheel to avoid an anthill '—Brahmans come down from four Indian breeds; they were first imported here from the USA in 1933. Droughtmasters are a Brahman cross, developed here. They've all adapted particularly to this part of the world for a variety of reasons. They're heat-and-parasite resistant, they're mobile, good foragers and they can survive on poor grass in droughts. They have a highly developed digestive system that provides efficient feed-conversion.'

'They sound amazing.'

'There's more,' he said with a grin. 'The fact that they're resistant to or tolerant of parasites means they don't require chemical intervention, so they're clean and green,' he said humorously. 'The cows are good mothers; they produce plenty of milk and they have small calves, so birthing is usually easy, and they're renowned for protecting their calves. All of that—' he waved a hand '—means they require minimum management. In answer to your question, that's why we don't need an army of staff.'

Holly looked around at the now undulating countryside they were driving through. It was quite rocky, she noticed, and dotted with anthills as well as spindly trees and scrub. The grass was long and spiky.

'But this is only one of your stations, isn't it?' she said.

'Yes, we have two more, roughly in this area, and

one in the Northern Territory.' He drew up and pointed. 'There you are—Brahmans.'

Holly stared at the cream and mainly brown cattle with black points. They were gathered around a dam. They had big droopy ears, sloe eyes, dewlaps and medium humps. 'They look so neat and smooth.'

'It's that smooth coat and their highly developed sweat glands that help them cope with the heat.'

'Do they come in any other colours?'

'Yes, grey with black points, but we don't have any greys here on Haywire.'

'It's so interesting!' She took some pictures then folded her arms and watched the cattle intently.

Brett Wyndham watched her for a long moment.

In her yellow singlet top, her jeans and no-nonsense shoes, she didn't look at all out of place in the landscape. In her enthusiasm, she looked even more apt for the setting; with her pale skin, that cloud of fair curls and no make-up, she was different and rather uniquely attractive.

He thought of her in her swimming costume only this morning: very slender, yes, but leggy with a kind of coltish grace that he'd found quite fascinating. Then again, in all her incarnations he'd found her fascinating…

He stirred and glanced at his watch. 'Seen enough?'

Holly turned her head and their gazes clashed for a moment. She felt her skin prickle as an unspoken communication seemed to flow between them, one of mutual awareness.

Then he looked away and switched on the engine, and the moment was broken, but the awareness of Brett

Wyndham didn't leave her as they bounced over the uneven terrain back to the compound.

Quite unaware that her thoughts echoed his thoughts, she remembered him all sleek and tall in the waters of Palm Cove that morning. She recalled how easily he'd picked her up in his arms and carried her up the beach. She shivered inwardly as she remembered the feel of her skin on his skin.

Brett parked the ute outside the compound fence and pointed out of his window. Holly followed the line of his finger and saw three emus treading with stately precision down the fenceline.

She breathed excitedly—not only in genuine interest, but because she was grateful to be relieved of her memories of the morning…

'It's already like a zoo here,' she told him.

They watched for a while, then got out, and he led the way to the cabin she'd been allotted.

'You've got half an hour before pre-dinner drinks. Would you like to freshen up?' he asked.

'Thanks,' she said gratefully.

'This is a guest cabin. By the way, there's plenty of hot water.'

'Lovely,' Holly murmured,

He turned away, but turned back. 'Oh, there should be a functioning torch in there—use it when you're walking around the compound at night. There could be frogs. Or snakes.'

'Frogs I can handle,' Holly said. 'Snakes I'm not too keen on, but I guess usual practice—make a bit of a noise as you move about so the ground vibrates and otherwise beat a hasty retreat?'

'Good thinking; they're not common,' he agreed.

'That's nice to hear,' Holly said with some humour.

'We *are*—almost—beyond the black stump.'

'Now you tell me,' she quipped, and closed herself into the cabin.

She immediately discovered that Haywire might be remote, and might resemble a safari camp in some respects, but its cabins were sturdy, beautifully appointed and had very modern bathrooms.

The double bed had a sumptuous thick-looking but light-as-air doona covered in an intricately embroidered cream-linen cover, with four matching pillows. It was also a four-poster bed. There were paintings on the dark-green walls and the carpet was the kind your feet sank into in a soft sea-green. There was a beautiful cedar chest, two armchairs and a delicate writing-desk with cabriole legs. The bedside lamps had porcelain bases and coral-pink linen shades.

The bathroom was a symphony of white tiles, black floor and shiny chrome taps. Lime-green and lemon-yellow was echoed not only in the towels and the robes that hung behind the door but in the cakes of soap and toiletries all provided in glass bottles, with an ornamental 'H' for Haywire entwined with a 'W' for Wyndham.

She took a hot shower and changed into a pair of clean jeans and a long-sleeved blue blouse that matched her eyes. She thought about wearing her heavy shoes as protection against any snakes on the loose, but decided her feet needed a change, and slipped them into her ballet pumps.

As usual she spent a few minutes grappling with her hair; she'd washed it, but in the end merely pushed her fingers through it and left it to its own devices. She'd discovered that very few people with curly hair actually appreciated it, whilst many who did not have it thought it would be marvellous to do so. She grimaced at her reflection as she recalled the agonies in her teens when she would have given her eye teeth to have straight smooth hair.

That Brett Wyndham didn't seem averse to it occurred to her—and, since she had five minutes to play with, she sat down in one of the armchairs and thought about him.

In particular she thought about that charged little moment out in the ute when their gazes had locked and she'd been so aware of everything about him. Not only that, but she'd sensed it was mutual. Where could it ever lead? she wondered. There was something about him she couldn't put her finger on. Yes, she'd decided he was a loner—it was pretty obvious he lived the kind of life that didn't go well with domestic ties—but was there something even more remote about him?

If so, did it come from his broken engagement to Natasha Hewson or did it go deeper than that?

She frowned as she suddenly remembered what he'd said this morning about going into areas he didn't want to go to. What could that be about? she wondered as she cast her mind over all the material she'd collected from him the previous evening. None of it had been especially riveting, mostly family history, history of the area and some anecdotes... *Hang on!*

She paused her thoughts as it struck her that those

few anecdotes from his formative years had included his brother Mark, his sister Sue, his mother, who was a doctor, and his grandparents but not one word about his father. Wasn't that a little strange?

She shook her head, more than ever conscious that Brett Wyndham was an enigma. She also had to concede that there was a spark of chemistry between them—more than a spark. She couldn't deny there were times when she loved his company, even though he'd so incensed her at the beginning, but she also couldn't deny her wariness.

Of course, some of that was to do with what had once happened to her, but who would wittingly fall in love with an enigmatic loner? She posed the question to herself.

CHAPTER FIVE

SHE didn't encounter any snakes or frogs on the way to dinner. In fact, Bella came to meet her as she opened her door and escorted her.

'You are a lovely dog,' she said to Bella as they arrived, then, 'Wow—this looks amazing!'

Oil lamps hung from the rafters, shedding soft light. The table was set with colourful, linen place mats, pewter and crystal, and a bowl of swamp lilies. There was a bottle of champagne in an ice bucket, and there was the tantalizing smell of roast beef in the air.

Brett had obviously showered too; his hair was damp and spiky and he'd changed into khaki trousers and a checked shirt. He looked devastatingly attractive, Holly thought privately.

'Champagne?' he invited, lifting the bottle by its neck and starting to ease the foil off.

'Yes, please.' Holly looked around. 'I must say this is amazingly civilized for beyond the black stump.'

'We do our best. Champagne, Sarah?' he called.

'No, thanks,' Sarah called back. 'I'm in the midst of dishing up; I'll have one later.'

'Has it always been like this—Haywire?' Holly

asked, and lifted her glass in a response to Brett's silent toast.

'More or less,' he replied and shrugged. 'Ever since I can remember, although the cabins have been renovated and more mod cons put in. But I never wanted to change *this*.' He gestured comprehensively.

'I'm so glad; it's magic,' Holly said enthusiastically.

Not a great deal later Holly said to Sarah, 'That was fantastic,' as she put her knife and fork together and pushed her plate away. 'Not only roast beef but Yorkshire pudding.'

'I am a Yorkshire lass,' Sarah revealed as she stood up and began clearing plates. 'There's fruit and cheese to come, and coffee.'

'Please, let me help,' Holly offered.

'No way! I am being paid to do this. You and Brett relax,' Sarah ordered.

Holly breathed a little frustratedly. She didn't really want to be left alone with Brett—well, she did and she didn't, she decided. But she felt tense about it; she felt jittery.

On the other hand, she didn't want to force herself on Sarah in the kitchen. Some cooks hated having their space invaded with offers of help.

She got up, but stood undecided beside her chair, and it seemed to show in her face.

She saw Brett watching her rather narrowly and wondered what he was thinking. Then she realized, as his dark gaze flicked up and down her figure, that he was thinking of her in a particular context—the awareness that continued to spring up between them—and she felt herself colour; she turned away, biting her lip.

He was the one who solved the problem. He said, 'I've got a few things to do, a few calls to make. Why don't you look through the albums? It might give you more background material.'

She turned back. 'Albums?'

He indicated the library area and some thick albums arranged on a teak table. A comfortable armchair stood beside the table and a lamp above it shed light.

'There are photos going way back; there are visitors' comments and press cuttings.'

'Oh, thank you! I will,' she said eagerly, but didn't miss the ironic little glance he cast her. In fact, it caused her to bridle as she stared back.

But he only shrugged and drew her attention to a drawer in the table that contained pens and paper, if she wanted to make notes.

'Thank you,' she said stiffly. Feeling foolish, which didn't sit well with her, she waved her hands and recommended that he go away and leave her alone.

'By all means, Miss Harding,' he said with soft sarcasm. 'By all means.'

Holly ground her teeth.

An hour later she looked up as he came back into the library area, then put her pen down and stretched.

'Finished?' he enquired.

'No. They're fascinating—I could go on for hours, but I won't. Thanks very much.' She closed the album she'd been working on and stood up. 'I think bed might be a good idea. I seem to have done an awful lot today,' she said with evident humour.

'I'll walk you to your cabin,' he murmured.

'I can walk myself.' But she paused, feeling recalcitrant and juvenile. What could happen between here and her cabin? 'OK. Thanks.'

They called goodnight to Sarah, who was watching a DVD, and set off. In the event, there were no snakes, but there was a flying fox. As Brett opened her cabin door and reached in to switch on the light, it swooped down on Holly.

It startled her so much she dropped her torch, gave a yelp and with an almighty shudder sought refuge in Brett's arms.

The creature flew into the cabin, then straight out again.

'It's only a flying fox,' he said, holding her close, though, and flipping off the light. 'It was the light.'

'Only a flying fox!' she repeated incredulously. 'Aren't they responsible for the Lyssa virus or the Hendra virus—or both?'

'It didn't actually touch you, Holly.' He passed a hand over her hair then closed the cabin door.

She shuddered again. 'Can you imagine it getting caught in my hair? Yuck!'

'Some people love them.'

'Not in their hair, I bet they don't. Look, I'm not keen on them; snakes, spiders, rats and frogs I can manage to stay sane about—flying foxes, not!'

He laughed down at her then bent his head to kiss her.

Holly was taken completely by surprise, but it felt

so good, she was immediately riveted and all her fears seemed to melt away.

Then some common sense prevailed and she drew away a little.

'We shouldn't be doing this,' she whispered.

'We've been wanting to do it all day,' he countered.

'I…' She swallowed. 'The thing is, I'm here to do a job and I really need to concentrate on that. So.' She managed to look up at him humorously. 'Thanks for being here, otherwise I could have really freaked out! But now I'll say goodnight.'

He released her promptly, although with a crooked little smile. 'All right. Don't switch the light on until you're closed in.' He turned away and left her.

Holly closed herself into the cabin and stood in the dark for a long moment with her hand to her mouth.

The next morning, after breakfast, he had a surprise for her.

She'd greeted him cautiously, but he'd been casual and friendly and they'd eaten breakfast companionably.

Then he recommended that she bring a hat and sunscreen, along with her camera, and meet him at the holding-paddock gate.

When she got there, there were two saddled horses tied to the fence.

'I'm sorry,' he said. 'I couldn't rustle up a camel or a donkey.'

Holly groaned. 'Thank heavens! But I have to tell you that, although I have ridden horses before, I'm not much of a rider—I usually get led.'

'No problem.' He produced a long rein out of his

saddle bag and attached it to one of the horses' bridles. 'Up you get.' He put his hands around her waist and lifted her into the saddle.

'Where are we going?'

He mounted his horse with ease and clicked his tongue. As they set off, he said, 'We're putting in a new dam; I want to see the progress. It's a pleasant ride.'

'You're not going to gallop or do anything that'll contribute to me falling off?' she queried as she clutched her reins and tried to adjust herself to the motion as they broke into a trot.

'Nope. Just relax. Are you always this nervous when you're on a job?'

'Often with good cause, believe me,' she said a shade tartly. 'I've even been known to get off and walk, but I do always get there in the end.'

Brett Wyndham grimaced.

'What?' she asked with conspicuous hauteur.

He laughed softly. 'I believe you. You're a stubborn one, Holly Golightly; that I don't doubt. OK. Let's see if we can enjoy this ride.'

An hour later they reached the dam sight, and to Holly's surprise she had enjoyed the ride. They'd stopped a couple of times, once on a rocky crest that had afforded them a sweeping view of the countryside, and once beside a salt lick.

Both times she'd dismounted and asked a lot of questions. By the time they reached the dam, she was confident enough of her horse not to need the leading rein, and she was genuinely charmed when Brett lit a small fire and boiled the billy he had in his saddle bag.

She reached into hers as instructed and withdrew some damper Sarah had baked to go with their tea.

'A real bush picnic,' she enthused as she sat on a rock and fanned herself with her hat. 'Oh—I can see a bulldozer over there. And a camp—but not a soul in sight!'

'Yes.' Brett squatted beside the fire and put a few more sticks on it. 'They usually work two weeks on, one week off. I wanted to check it all out on their off-week. Ready for your tea?' He poured boiling water onto a teabag in an enamel mug and handed it to her.

'Mmm…I'm looking forward to this. Thank you. But I don't see any cattle.'

'We rotate paddocks; this one's resting.'

'I see. How long…?'

But he interrupted her to give her all the information she was about to ask for about the paddocks, and more besides.

Holly had to laugh, although a little self-consciously, when he'd finished. 'Sorry, I'm asking too many questions, but it is interesting.'

He sent her a thoughtful look. She seemed to be completely unfazed by the heat and the flies; she seemed quite unaware that she had a dirty smudge on her face, or that her hands were grimy, that her hair was plastered to her head or that her shirt was streaked with sweat.

'You'd make a good countrywoman,' he said at last.

Holly tried the damper and pronounced it delicious. 'I'm insatiably curious,' she said. 'That's my problem.'

He looked thoughtful, but he didn't comment. When

they'd finished their tea, he put the fire out carefully, they mounted again and went to explore the dam
workings.

Two hours later they cantered back into the holding
paddock and Brett suggested a swim in the pool.

'Sounds heavenly,' Holly said in a heartfelt way,
and went to change into her togs. She was on her way
to the pool when it occurred to her that Sarah wasn't
around, and that she hadn't been quite her cheerful self
at breakfast. She hesitated then went to knock on her
cabin door.

Sarah opened it eventually and was full of apologies.
'I'm sorry, I'll get stuck into lunch—I've just got a touch
of sinus, but I've taken something. Makes me feel a bit
sleepy, though.'

Holly studied the other girl's pale face and the dark
rings under her eyes. 'Oh, no,' she said. 'You go back
to bed. I can handle lunch!'

'I wouldn't dream of it,' Sarah replied, but her gaze
fastened on something over Holly's shoulder. Holly
turned round to see that Brett was standing behind her.
Before Sarah got a chance to say anything, she explained
the situation to him and finished by saying, 'I could
make lunch easily.'

'Done,' Brett said with authority. 'You do as you're
told, Sarah.'

'I should be better in time to make dinner,' Sarah
said anxiously.

'We'll see about that,' her boss replied, and reached
out to rumple Sarah's hair. 'Take it easy,' he advised
her.

Sarah sighed and looked relieved.

* * *

In the event Holly made both lunch and dinner. They had a swim in the pool before lunch, then Brett poured them a gin and tonic each—a fitting aperitif for the middle of a hot day, he told her—while she made open cold roast beef sandwiches with hot English mustard and salad.

They took their drinks and lunch to a table beside the pool beneath a shady tree.

Holly had put her peasant blouse on over her togs but Brett had added nothing to his board shorts. Bella lay beside them, gently indicating that she'd be happy to clean up any scraps. The bush beyond the fence was shimmering in the heat and vibrating with insect life.

'How do you manage to leave this place so often?' Holly asked.

'Don't kid yourself,' Brett responded. 'You can feel isolated up here.'

'But you can drive out, can't you?'

'Sure, but it's a long way on a rough road.'

Holly sipped her drink. 'Do your sister and brother like it up here?'

'From time to time, but they don't really have cattle in their blood. Neither does Aria. She doesn't really enjoy roughing it.' He grimaced then elaborated. 'She's the girl Mark's marrying.'

'What's she like?'

Brett considered and gave Bella the last bit of his sandwich. 'Very beautiful. She has long blonde hair, a striking figure. She and Natasha make a good pair, come to think of it, although Nat's a redhead.' He paused. 'My ex-fiancée.'

Holly's mind fled back to the dinner party she'd

witnessed at Palm Cove. Unless there were two stunning redheads in his life, had the one she'd seen been his ex-fiancée? If so, did that mean they were still friends?

'No curiosity on that subject, Miss Harding?' he queried, a shade dryly.

Holly shrugged and looked away. 'I'm sure it's out of bounds, and besides, its none of my business.'

'True.' He looked reflective. 'Anyway, Aria is a biochemist and actually very nice, although something of a meddler.' He looked briefly heavenwards. 'But since Mark's a computer genius they have similar lifestyles in common.'

Holly looked around. 'So all this falls to you? I mean all the responsibility, the planning and so on.'

'Yes.' He sat back and crossed his hands behind his head.

'It must be quite a handful, combining it with your other work.'

'More or less what I've been thinking for a while now,' he agreed with a wry little smile. He sobered. 'But it's in my blood. Just as you inherited your father's writing gene, I must have inherited my f—' He stopped abruptly.

Holly waited but found she was holding her breath.

'Much as I don't care to admit it,' he said finally, 'I must have inherited my father's gene for cattle and the land.'

Holly released her breath slowly. Although the thought chased through her mind that she'd been right—there had been something between Brett and his father—she was mindful of his warning about going into things he didn't want go into.

'So it's something you really love,' she said instead. 'I can understand that.'

He looked at her penetratingly. 'You can?'

'I think so. It's probably unfair to say there are more challenges out here than in suburban life, but to me anyway these open spaces are not only exciting—' she looked up at the wide arc of blue, blue sky above '—they're liberating. I guess that's what motivated my father and may have come down to me.'

'You really mean that, don't you?' He sat up.

Holly nodded, then grimaced. 'Probably easy enough to say. So. What's on this afternoon?'

He eyed her, sitting so relaxed in her chair in her peasant blouse with its pretty embroidery, her legs long and bare and her hair curling madly.

What's on this afternoon? he repeated to himself. *What would you say, Miss Harding, if I told you I'd very much like to take you to bed? I'd love to strip your togs from your body and explore those slender lines and delicate curves. I'd like to touch you and make those pink lips part in surprise and pleasure, those blue eyes widen in wonder...*

It was a disturbance over the fence in the holding paddock that drew his attention away from Holly—saved by the bell, he thought dryly. He saw that his foreman, Kane, had arrived back from the fencing trip with his two offsiders.

But as his gaze came back to Holly, he saw that she was staring at him with her lips parted, her eyes wide—all in some perplexity.

His lips twisted. 'Why don't you relax? I've got some things to discuss with Kane. I may take him back to the dam to show him what I want done, so I could be tied up all afternoon.'

'Uh, all right,' Holly responded after a moment. 'I can do some work anyway.' She hesitated. 'If Sarah's still not well would you like me to cook dinner?'

'Thanks.' He stood up. 'That would be great.'

Holly withdrew her gaze from the physical splendour of Brett Wyndham in his board shorts. 'Um, do I cook for Kane and the others?'

'No. They'll cater for themselves in their quarters. See you later.' And he walked away.

Holly cleared up their lunch and retreated to her cabin, where she admitted to herself that she was somewhat bothered and bewildered. Or bewitched.

She lay down on the bed and stared at the ceiling, feeling like a star-struck teenager, she admitted as she pulled a pillow into her arms. So, what to do about it?

No answer presented itself and she fell asleep.

It was starting to cool down when she re-emerged, showered and once again changed in her blouse and jeans.

She checked on Sarah first and took her a pot of tea and a snack—all she wanted. She persuaded her to stay where she was, assuring her she was quite able to handle dinner.

A couple of hours later, with the oil lamps lit and the table set attractively again, Brett put down his knife and fork and said, 'You can cook. Another gene from your father?'

Holly's face dimpled into a smile as she glanced at the remains of the golden-brown lasagne she'd prepared, along with a fresh green salad and some warm rolls.

'No. The cooking gene comes from my mother, in case you thought I was all my father's doing.'

Brett lay back in his chair and studied her. He had also showered and had changed into a clean khaki shirt and beige chinos. 'What does come to mind...' He twirled his wine glass. 'Is the fact that you'd make someone a really handy wife.'

Holly looked put out, although there was glint of laughter in her eyes. 'That's not exactly a compliment, Mr Wyndham,' she said gravely.

'Sorry,' He grimaced. 'As well as a very attractive wife, of course.'

'That's a bit better!' Holly approved. 'But I don't think I'd make a good wife, actually.'

'Why not?'

She gathered their plates. 'Oh, I don't know.' She shrugged and stood up.

He rose too and told her to sit down. 'I'll do this.'

Holly sank back and watched him clear the table. He came back and topped up their wine glasses. 'Why not?' he asked again.

She looked at him and looked away. She stroked Bella's head. Somehow the dog must have gauged her inner distress with the subject, because Bella had risen and put her head on Holly's lap. Despite her inner distress, there was something else, something new. For the first time she wanted to explain why she was the way she was.

It was to do with this man, she thought. Because he moved her, whether she liked it or not...

She took a deep breath. 'A couple of years ago I fell madly in love,' she said quietly. 'What I didn't know was that he was a married man. And I only got to know it when his wife started stalking me.'

Brett stopped with his wine glass poised in his hand, then he slowly put it down. 'I'm sorry. *Seriously* stalking you?'

'I thought so. She wrote threatening letters, she threatened me over the phone, she turned up at work, she harassed my mother—she threw a brick through my car window once. It got to the stage where I was looking over my shoulder all the time, even scared to go out.'

'She sounds crazy,' he said.

Holly shrugged. 'I'll probably never know whether it was the cause or the effect of her husband's philandering, but it left me with several complexes. Strangely, although she scared me silly at times, I felt a streak of sympathy for *her*, whereas I could have killed her husband for putting me in that position. You could say I fell off cloud nine with a huge bump.'

She looked away and for a moment tears glittered in her eyes.

'Go on,' he murmured eventually.

'I couldn't believe I'd been so thoroughly taken in by him. I can only—I'd just lost my father, who meant the world to me, so I was depressed and so on when I met him.'

'He was still living with her?'

'No, he'd moved out, so I had no reason to suspect he was married. But I guess that's my number-one complex—a terrible lack of judgement on my part. Funnily enough, I'd never believed I was the kind of girl to be swept off her feet by a man.'

'Or vice versa—who does?'

Holly smiled bleakly. 'It doesn't help. Anyway, I'm very much on guard against that kind of thing happening to me again. And I'm terribly, terribly wary now of the maelstrom of emotions that can go with love and marriage.'

'Maybe she was a unhinged. Perhaps you struck a one-in-a-million situation?' he suggested.

'Or maybe she just felt herself to be a woman scorned. Maybe she felt she couldn't live without him; they had two children. Maybe she just felt desperate; I don't know,' Holly said.

'What happened to them?'

'He went back to her and they moved overseas.' Holly fiddled with her napkin then looked straight into his eyes.

'But for a few months I was in serious trouble. I felt so guilty, even though I hadn't known about her. I was a nervous wreck—I still sometimes break out into a sweat and think I'm being followed. But my mother finally persuaded me to get some counselling and that's when I realized only I could get myself out of it. So I plunged into my work and the harder, even the more dangerous it was, the better.'

'And now?'

Holly rubbed her hands together. 'For the most part, fine, but still terribly wary of men and love and marriage—and my own lack of judgement.'

'I see.' He finished his wine. 'I guess that explains your aversion to *chemistry*.'

Holly bit her lip. Of course, he was quite right. The only thing was, she hadn't had any problems with "chemistry" after that disastrous affair until *he* had come into her life. Well, she'd been perfectly capable of stonewalling it without feeling it herself, but that was not the case now.

She looked across at him. 'My mistrust of it, yes. But I can't say it hasn't happened.'

'Between us?'

'Yes,' she whispered. She gestured a little helplessly. 'But you—you're… This is business, *serious* business for me anyway. I need to get this interview right. If I don't, you'll can it or my editor will.' She said with sudden passion, 'I need to make it vibrant and compelling. I can't do that if I'm—distracted.'

He stared at her with his lips twitching.

'What?' she asked huskily.

'You are on the horns of a dilemma.'

'If you're going to laugh at me…'

'I'm not,' he interrupted. 'Although that did strike me as, well, probably the least of our problems.'

Holly felt herself blush. She said honestly, 'You're right. I don't know where that bit came from.'

'Come and see the moon.' He stood up, came round to her and held out his hand.

She looked up at him. 'Where did *that* come from?'

He smiled. 'The moon? It just struck me, it's full tonight. See?' He pointed out towards the east.

Holly gasped at the orange globe rising above the tree line. 'Oh! How beautiful.' She got up.

'Mmm…' He took her hand and led her out onto the lawn.

Holly was transfixed as the moon rose, and in the process lost some of its orange radiance and shrunk a bit. She shivered. Days out in the savannah might be hot, but the nights were very cold, and she hadn't put on her jumper.

Brett put his arms around her. She couldn't help herself, and she snuggled up to him.

'Maybe this says it all,' he murmured, and started to kiss her.

Her lips quivered, but it seemed to her that her senses would no longer be dictated by her mind. They clamoured for his touch; they were lit by the feel of him, tall and hard against her, and tantalized by the pure essence of man she was breathing in.

She loved the press of his fingers against her skin; she loved the way they explored the nape of her neck and behind her ears while he kept his other hand around her waist.

But a skerrick of common sense claimed her and she raised her hands to put them on his chest. 'We ought to stop and think,' she breathed. 'This could be very dangerous.'

He lifted his head. 'Why? It has nothing to do with anyone but us, and we couldn't be in more agreement at the moment if we tried.'

Holly made a strange little sound in her throat. He stared down at her mouth in the moonlight and started to kiss her again.

She was almost carried away with delight when he stopped and raised his head to listen.

She came out of her enchanted trance with a start as she too heard footsteps. 'Sarah,' she breathed. 'I'd forgotten about her. She must be feeling a bit better—hungry, maybe!'

'We'll go to your…'

'No! I need to go and see if she's OK.' Holly stood on tiptoe and kissed him swiftly. 'Thanks for listening.' She sped off back towards the house.

Brett said something unrepeatable under his breath then looked down to see Bella sitting beside him. 'Come to sympathize, old girl? Well, what would you say if I told you that Holly Harding could be the right one for me? She's taken to Haywire as if she was born to it; she could be running the place, but of course it's not only that. She's becoming more and more desirable. But do I want a wife? It's hard to put down roots without one. How good would I be with a wife, though?

CHAPTER SIX

THERE was a triple knock on Holly's door before sunrise the next morning.

She'd been hovering on the edge of wakefulness for a while and she jerked upright, scrambled out of bed and went to open the door. 'What? Who? Why?' she breathed. 'Has something happened?'

'No.' It was Brett dressed in jeans and a jacket. 'Come and see the sunrise.'

'But I'm not even dressed!'

'Throw some warm clothes on, then; we haven't got much time.'

She hesitated then shrugged. 'OK.'

Ten minutes later she joined him in the ute.

She'd thrown on some slouchy trousers and a jacket and she was finger-plaiting her hair. They bumped over some rough ground for a few minutes then came to a lip in the ground, as far as she could see in the headlights.

Brett pulled up and switched the ute off. 'Won't be long now. Come and sit on the bonnet.

Holly did as she was bid, and slowly the rim of the horizon started to lighten. As it did the chill breeze that had seen her wrap her arms around herself dropped.

With gathering speed, the darkness faded and she was looking down a long valley; all the colours of the landscape—the burnt umber and olive greens, the forest greens and splashes of amber—started to come alive as the sun reached the horizon.

It was so beautiful in the crystal-clear cool air, and alive in every little detail. She found she was holding her breath as she watched a wedge-tail eagle planing the thermals. Then as the sun climbed higher, that particular vividness of early dawn faded a little, and she sighed wistfully.

'Thank you for that,' she whispered, as if she was afraid of breaking the spell by talking aloud.

He merely nodded and got off the bonnet, but only to reach into the ute for a thermos flask and two cups.

The coffee he poured from the flask was full-bodied and aromatic. 'I thought you might be cross with me for dragging you out of bed.'

'No. Well...' Holly grinned. 'That may have been my first tiny reaction.' She sipped her coffee and sniffed appreciatively. 'Smells so good!'

He climbed back onto the bonnet. 'So you slept well?'

'I did. I...' She hesitated and thought of the tussle she'd had with herself before she'd been able to fall asleep. 'I did decide I needed to apologize.'

He raised an eyebrow at her. 'What for?'

Holly chewed her lip. 'This is not that easy to say but I seem to have developed the habit of—kissing you— and, uh, sloping off.'

'You have,' he agreed after a moment.

Holly looked slightly put out.

'What did you expect me to say?' He drained his coffee and put his cup down.

'I didn't expect you to agree quite so readily. And there are reasons for it, of course.'

'Of course,' he echoed. 'Such as, we just can't seem to help ourselves? That's what promotes it in the first place, at least.'

Holly wrapped her hands around her mug and was considering her reply when he went on, 'Then you get cold feet.'

'Well, I do! Why wouldn't I?'

He tilted her chin, observed the indignation in her eyes and smiled slightly. 'I could be going too fast. Should we just be friends for today?' He released her chin and put his arm around her shoulders.

Holly opened her mouth to ask him *what* he was going too fast towards, but she decided against it. She diagnosed one good reason for that: it felt so good to have his arm around her, and to contemplate a friendly day ahead, she didn't feel like debating anything.

'What else will we do today?' she enquired.

'I'm flying to Croydon for a meeting, cattle stuff. If you'd like to come, you could visit the old gold-rush museum and we could fly onto Karumba for lunch. Karumba is on the Gulf of Carpentaria.'

'Sounds great. I think I'd like that very much.'

She did.

She pottered around Croydon while he was in his meeting, she marvelled at the size of the Norman River from the air and she enjoyed a seafood basket on a thick, green lawn beneath shady trees. The Sunset Tavern at

Karumba Point sat on the mouth of the Norman River and overlooked the shimmering waters of the gulf.

'It must be magic at sunset,' she said idly.

'It is. Pity we can't stay, but I've got another meeting this afternoon at Haywire.' He stretched his legs out and clasped his hands behind his head.

'Never mind. It's been beautiful.'

He looked across at her. 'You're easy to please.'

'I don't think it's that. It *has* been great.' She pushed away her empty seafood-basket. 'So were the prawns.'

He laughed. 'Karumba is the headquarters of the gulf prawning-industry—they should be!'

Holly patted her stomach and sat back. That was when she noticed a couple of young women seated at a table nearby and how they were watching Brett with obvious fascination.

She grimaced mentally and felt some sympathy for them. Whether they knew who he was or not, *she* did. Thinking about him in his cargo pants and black sweat-shirt, with his ruffled dark hair and that eagle intensity at times in his dark eyes, and with his tall, streamlined physique, she had no difficulty picturing him engaging in dangerous exploits like shooting tranquilizer darts out of helicopters or parachuting into jungles.

Worse than that, she herself had not been immune from the effect of Brett Wyndham, although it had been designated a 'friendly' day. His hands on her waist when he'd lifted her down from the plane had sent shivers through her. Walking side by side with him had done the same.

Even doing those mundane things—not to mention laughing, chatting and sometimes being teased by him, channelled an awareness of him through her pores, both physical and mental.

I love him, she thought suddenly. *I love being with him. I love his height and his strength, his hands; I love breathing in his essence. But how can that be? It's only been a few days...*

She looked up suddenly to see him eyeing her with a question in his eyes.

'Sorry,' she murmured, going faintly pink. 'Did you say something?'

'Only—ready to go?'

'Oh. Yes. Whenever you are.'

'Something wrong?' His dark eyes scanned her intently.

'No,' she said slowly—but thought, *I don't know; I just don't know...*

Back at Haywire that afternoon, she took herself to task and forbade any more deep thinking on the subject of Brett Wyndham—in relation to her personally, that was. She went to work on her notes while Brett had his next meeting. She didn't ask what his business was, but two planes landed on the strip and he was closeted with the passengers for several hours.

She worked in her cabin, going over all the material she'd gathered, including the zoo details, and putting it into order.

She paused once; she was conscious of a lack, a hole in her story about Brett Wyndham, and realized it was the lack of any detail about his father. But there was another lack, she felt, brought on by her vision of him out at Karumba performing dangerous deeds. So far she had no details about his life as a vet in far-off exotic lands, and she would need that.

She made some notes then paused again and frowned. It occurred to her that if she were asked whether she could capture the essence of Brett Wyndham she would have to say no. There *was* something missing. But what made her think that? Some invisible barrier in him, drawn fairly and squarely so you couldn't cross it. The way just occasionally, when he was talking about his life, she sensed that he retreated and you knew without doubt you'd come to a no-go zone.

She realized she'd put it down to him being a genuine loner, but now she couldn't help wondering if there was more to it.

She shook her head as she wondered if it was her imagination. Then she put her pen down as she heard the noise of aircraft engines, and the two visiting planes taking off. Bella scratched on her door. She let her in and noticed a note attached to her collar with her name on it.

'Why, Bella,' she murmured. 'You clever girl!'

She smoothed the note open and digested the gist of it: a couple of the visitors had decided to stay overnight and would be picked up the following morning. Would Holly care to have dinner with them in about an hour?

Holly sent Bella back with an acceptance penned to the note. Then she went to find Sarah and offer her help, but Sarah was quite restored and wouldn't hear of it. So Holly showered and changed, this time into slim burgundy trousers and a pale-grey jumper over a white blouse.

* * *

It was a pleasant evening.

The two visitors were a couple from a neighbouring station and they proved to be good, lively company. It wasn't until ten-thirty that Holly excused herself and Brett walked her to her cabin.

'Had a nice day?' he enquired when they got there.

Holly turned to him impulsively. 'I've had a *lovely* day!'

'That's good. Ready to fly back to Cairns tomorrow?'

Holly grimaced. 'Yes, if not willing. But thanks for everything.' She glanced back towards the homestead where his guests were still sitting. 'You better get back. Goodnight.'

'Goodnight,' he echoed, but with an ironic little smile.

'I know what you're thinking,' she said, then could have shot herself.

'You do?' He raised an eyebrow at her.

She clicked her tongue in some exasperation and soldiered on. 'You're thinking *I'm* thinking that I've been saved by the bell!'

'Something like that,' he agreed. 'That the presence of visitors will prevent me from kissing you goodnight? But, since I've been on my best behaviour all day, and since it really has nothing to do with anyone else, you're wrong.'

And he put his hands around her waist, drew her into him and kissed her deeply.

Holly came up for air with her pulses hammering and her whole body thrilling to his touch, to the feel of him against her.

He put her away from him gently and smoothed the collar of her blouse. 'Don't put the light on until you're closed inside,' he advised. 'Goodnight.' And he turned away.

It took ages for Holly to fall asleep that night as she examined and re-examined her feelings; as she wondered about his, was conscious of a thrilling little sense of excitement. How could she have grown so close to him in such a short time? she asked herself. It was like a miracle, for her. But it wasn't only the physical attraction—although that was overwhelming enough—it was the powerful pull of his personality. It was as if he'd taken centre-stage in her life and she had no idea how to go on with that lynchpin removed…

Where would it all lead?

There was no opportunity for any personal interaction the next morning. The two guests were picked up after breakfast and then Brett and Kane were called to the home paddock for a colt with colic.

Holly watched the proceedings from the paddock fence as Brett worked to keep the horse on its feet whilst Kane prepared a drench. Once again she could see how good Brett was with animals as he soothed and walked the stricken horse and then administered the drench.

He came out of the paddock wearing khaki overalls, with sweat running down his face, and asked her if she was ready to leave. She nodded, said her goodbyes to Sarah and Bella and looked around. 'Bye, Haywire,' she murmured. 'You're quite a place.'

She hadn't realized that Brett was watching her thoughtfully while she'd said her goodbyes.

When they were alone, finally in the air, they didn't have much to say to each other at all, at first—until Brett made a detour and flew low over the ground to point out to her where he planned to locate the zoo.

'There's water.' He indicated several dams. 'There's good ground cover, but of course we'll have to feed by hand, so we'll establish several feed-stations.'

'There are no roads,' she said slowly.

'Not yet, and no fences, but that'll all come.'

'Are you planning to make it a tourist attraction?' she queried. 'I don't know if it's what you have in mind, but I read somewhere about a zoo that offered a camping ground as well. If you're thinking of an adopt-an-animal scheme, people might be interested in seeing their animals in the flesh, so to speak.'

He glanced at her. 'Good thinking.'

'It's a huge project.'

'Yes,' he agreed. 'But it needs to be done—I feel, anyway. OK.' The little plane lifted its nose and climbed. 'Back to the mundane—well, back to Cairns, anyway, and the wedding.'

But fate had other ideas for them. Not long after they reached their cruising altitude, the plane seemed to stutter, and Brett swore.

'What?' Holly asked with her heart in her mouth.

'I don't know,' he replied tersely as he scanned gauges and checked instruments. 'But it could be a blocked fuel-line. Listen, I'm going to bring her down.' He scanned the horizon now. 'Over there, as best I can.'

Her eyes nearly fell out on stalks. 'Over there'

appeared to be a dry river-bed. 'But we're in the middle of nowhere!'

'Better than what might be the alternative. I'm also going to put out all the appropriate distress signals and hope to get a response before we go down. Holly, just do exactly as I say and buckle in tightly. If anything happens to me, once we're on the ground get out as fast as you can in case the fuel tanks go up.'

She swallowed convulsively several times as he spoke into his radio and the plane lost altitude and stuttered again.

Expecting to nose-dive out of the sky any moment—not that she knew anything about the mechanics of flying—she had to admire his absolute concentration and the way he nursed the little plane down.

'All right, now duck your head and hold on tight,' he ordered. 'I'm bringing her in.'

Holly did just that as well as send up some urgent prayers for help, through the next terrifying, never-ending minutes.

They landed and hopped over the uneven sandy ground, slewing and skidding madly until they finally came to a halt with the nose about a metre from a huge gum-tree on the bank. A cloud of birds rose from the tree.

It had been like being in a dry washing-machine, for Holly. She'd been buffeted and bruised even within the confine of her seat belt. Her limbs had reacted like she'd been a rag doll being shaken, but all of a sudden everything was still and there was an unearthly quiet. Even the birds had stopped squawking.

She stared at the gum tree, so close, so solid, and

swallowed. Then she switched her gaze to Brett. He was slumped over the half steering-wheel with a bleeding gash on his forehead. After a frozen moment of panic for Holly, he lifted his head, shook it groggily and was galvanized into action.

'Out,' he ordered. 'It only takes some fuel to drip onto a hot pipe and we'll be incinerated.'

With an almost Herculean effort, he managed to open his door and climb out. He turned immediately and reached for Holly, manhandled her out of her seat and down onto the ground, where he took her hand and dragged her away from the plane.

They were both panting with exertion by the time he judged them far enough away to be safe; running through the sand of the riverbed had been almost impossible. Holly sank to her knees, then her bottom, her face scarlet, her chest heaving. Brett did the same.

They waited for a good half-hour in the shimmering heat of the river bed but the plane didn't explode. He told her he was going back to it to salvage whatever he could. He also told her to stay put.

'No,' she said raggedly. 'I can help.'

'Holly.' He looked down at her with blood running down his face. 'Please do as you're told, damn it!'

'No.' She reared up on her knees. 'I can help,' she repeated. 'And you can't stop me. Besides, you're bleeding—you could have concussion—'

'It's nothing,' he broke in impatiently.

'I'm coming. In fact, I'm going.' She got painfully to her feet and started staggering through the sand.

He swore quite viciously, then followed her.

Between them they managed to get their bags and two

blankets out of the plane. Brett also found a spare water-bottle strapped to a small drinking-fountain with a tube of plastic cups. He took out not only the spare bottle but the fountain itself. Then he discovered a few cardboard cartons with Haywire stencilled on their sides.

'I was probably meant to deliver these, but no-one mentioned it.'

'What's in them?' Holly breathed.

'No idea. Maybe soap powder—maybe not. We'll take them,' he said.

He also checked the radio, but it was dead, and the satellite phone was smashed. Just as he left the plane for the last time, the starboard wheel-strut collapsed suddenly, tilting it to an unnatural angle and crumpling the starboard wing into the ground.

They froze and waited with bated breath but nothing more happened.

'When is it completely safe?' she asked shakily.

He put an arm round her shoulder. 'If it was going to happen, it would probably have happened by now.' He put his other arm around her. 'Holly.' He stopped and put his other arm round her. 'How are you?'

She tried to break free but he held her closer, and it was only then that she realized she was shaking like a leaf and not quite in control of herself. 'I—I'm sorry,' she stammered. 'It's reaction, I guess. But I'll be fine; just give a me a few moments.'

'Of course.' He held her very close and stroked her hair until she stopped shaking.

'How do you feel now?'

It was a few hours later and the sun was starting to slip

away. The constraint that had had them in its grip earlier in the day had melted away under the circumstances.

'Oh, fine,' Holly responded. 'Thank you. You?'

They'd made themselves as comfortable as possible in the creek bed not far from the plane. Brett was leaning back against a smooth rock. There was a tree growing out from the bank, giving them shade. They'd pegged out in the sand a bright-orange plastic sheet with a V on it, which they'd got from the plane, where it would be most visible from the air.

He grimaced. 'I've got a headache that would kill a cow.' He touched his fingers gingerly to the cut on his forehead that Holly had cleaned as well as she'd been able to.

The packages for Haywire had proved a godsend. They contained packets of biscuits, some self-opening tins of luncheon ham, packets of dates and raisins, six tins of sardines, six tubes of condensed milk and one cardboard carton of white wine.

An odd mixture, he'd commented when they'd broken them out, but at least it was not soap powder, so they wouldn't starve.

She'd agreed ruefully.

They'd also found a small axe and a gas firelighter.

Now, as she watched the sun slipping away, she said, 'It looks as if we'll have to spend the night here.'

'Yes.' He shrugged. 'I doubt if it will be more than a night. But it takes time to co-ordinate a search and hard to do in the dark.'

She looked around and shivered. 'It's a big country.'

He studied her dirty, rather tense face. 'Come here.'

She hesitated then crawled over and leant back beside him. He put an arm round her.

'I'm really worried about my mother,' she said. 'She'll be devastated when she hears this news.'

'Yes.' He said nothing more for a long moment, then, 'You do realize you have me at your mercy, don't you, Holly?' He brushed his lips against her hair.

'Well, I certainly wouldn't take advantage of you with a headache, if that's what you mean,' she returned with some humour.

'Pity about that,' he drawled, then relented as she looked at him incredulously. 'What I meant was, we could talk—fill in the gaps, go on with the interview.'

'Now? But I'm not at all organized.'

'I wouldn't have thought it would take a girl who handled a crash-landing in the middle of nowhere with aplomb long to organize herself.'

'It wasn't all aplomb.'

'Believe me, one little attack of the shakes is very close to aplomb.'

She considered. 'Well, I've got a good memory, so I'll rely on that. Oh!' She put a hand to her mouth. 'My laptop. I didn't even think to check if it got smashed. But hang on...' She fumbled in one of her pockets and with a cry of triumph produced a flash key. 'Safe and sound.'

'You back everything up on that and keep it on your person at all times?' he guessed.

She nodded vigorously. 'Bitter, if not to say heart-breaking experience has taught me that. OK. Uh, I was thinking only yesterday that we haven't touched on any of your exploits to do with saving endangered species. I'm sure readers would find that riveting. And do you have a favourite animal?'

He thought for a while. 'Yes—giraffe. There's nothing like seeing them cross a plain with that rocking-horse rhythm, or staring down at you from above the crown of a tree. I'm very keen on giraffe—or Twiga, which is their Swahili name.'

She chuckled and led him on to talk about some of the successes he'd had as an endangered-species expert. Then their talk turned general until he asked her about her childhood.

She told him about her adventures with her father and couldn't prevent the love and admiration she'd felt for her father shining through. 'I miss him every day of my life. Is your father alive—?' She stopped and bit her lip.

'No.'

'Your mother?'

'No.'

'I'm sorry,' she said.

'You don't need to be sorry on my father's account,' he said dryly.

Holly took an unexpected breath and wondered if he would enlarge on what she was pretty sure was the thorny subject of his father. But he said no more, and she regretted the fact that they had somehow lost their sense of easy camaraderie, so she took another tack.

'How *do* you combine your lifestyle—travelling the world and so on—with running a grazing empire? And it's more than that, isn't it? You've branched out into mining, transport, even a shipping line for live-cattle exports amongst other things. Or does it all run itself?'

She felt a jolt of laughter run through him and breathed a secret little sigh of relief.

'No, it doesn't.'

'They say you're a billionaire,' she observed. 'They say you're responsible for tripling the family fortune.'

He shrugged. 'I told you, in some ways I'm a quintessential cattle man. It's in my blood, so some of it comes naturally. I'm also very attached to this country.' He looked around. 'And I did set out to prove something to myself—that when I took over I'd never allow the empire to go backwards.' He paused, pushed himself upright and looked down at her. 'Do you realize you have a dirty face?' He touched the tip of her nose.

Holly grimaced as she thought, *subject closed.* She said, 'If you had any idea how battered as well as dirty I *feel.*' She looked around. 'There wouldn't be any pools in this river bed, do you think?'

'There could be. There could be tributaries with some water in them, it was a fairly good wet season, but there'll also be crocs.'

'Croc… Crocodiles?' she stammered.

'Uh-huh. Mostly fresh-water ones, usually safe, but enough to give you a fright. And it's not completely unknown for the odd salt-water croc to find its way up here. They are not safe.'

'I see. OK,' she said judiciously. 'I'm happy to stay dirty.'

He frowned. 'You also said battered, but you told me you were fine earlier. Where…?'

She held up a hand. 'I am fine. Just a bit shook up. It's

also starting to get cold—that might be making me feel my age,' she said humorously. 'Don't old cowboys feel every mended bone when there's a chill in the air?'

'I don't know.' He looked rueful. 'But we should make some preparations. I don't want to light a fire— the breeze is blowing towards the plane now—so our best bet is to wear as much of our clothing as we can.'

Holly had inspected their bags earlier. Hers had mostly contained clothes, his had yielded a few useful items other than clothes: a serious penknife with all sorts of attachments, a small but powerful pair of binoculars, a compass and a torch. And they both had wind cheaters fortunately, for later when the temperature dropped.

'All right.' She got up. 'But I do have to go on a little walkabout. I'll add some clothes at the same time. I presume if I'm not close to water I'm safe?'

'Relatively,' he replied. 'But don't go far, and stamp around a bit. There could be snakes.'

Holly swore under her breath.

When she returned, he'd laid out a meal. He'd cut up one of the tinned hams and, together with biscuits, dates and raisins, he'd set it all out on two pieces of cardboard roughly shaped as plates. And he'd poured two plastic cups of wine.

He handed her his pocket knife and said he was happy to use his fingers.

They ate companionably in the last of the daylight, then the dark. He told her about some of the safaris he'd been on and the electronic-tagging system he'd been involved with that tracked animals.

She got so involved in his stories, she might have

been in Africa or Asia with him, experiencing the triumphs and the disasters he'd encountered.

He also poured them a second, then a third, cup of wine.

'This will send me to sleep,' she murmured. 'Or make me drunk, as well as give me a hangover.'

She didn't see the acute little glance he beamed her way.

'I doubt the hangover bit,' he said. 'It's very light, but it might be an idea to get settled now. How about we scoop some sand about to make a bit of a hollow and something to rest our heads on?'

'OK. You hold the torch and I'll—'

'No. *You* hold the torch and I'll—'

'But I can—'

'For once in your life, just do as you're told, Holly Harding!'

She subsided, then chuckled suddenly.

'I probably look quite amusing,' he said as he scooped sand. 'But you don't have to laugh.'

'I'm not laughing at you,' she told him.

'Who, then?'

She waved a hand. 'It just seems a very long way from society weddings, balls and so on— Oh!' She put a hand to her mouth. 'When was your first pre-wedding party?'

'Tomorrow. Nothing we can do about it,' he said with a grimace.

'Perhaps they'll cancel it because you haven't turned up?'

'Perhaps. Not that I would wish it on them—having

to cancel it—but the more concerned people are about us, the sooner they'll start organizing a search.'

'Of course,' she said eagerly, then sat back again. 'What was I saying? Yes, it's actually rather lovely. Look at the stars,' she marveled, and hiccupped. 'Told you,' she added.

'Listen, take the torch if you need another bathroom call—don't go too far—and then let's go to bed, Miss Harding.'

'Roger wilco, Mr Wyndham!'

When she came back, he'd lined the hollow that he'd scooped with the cardboard of the cartons and the paper the foodstuffs had been wrapped in. As they settled themselves, he draped the rest of their clothes over them, then the two blankets.

She slept for about three hours, curled up beside him with his arm protectively over her.

Then she woke, and it wasn't so lovely any more. It was freezing. At first she had no idea where she was, then there was something large moving around on the edge of the creek bed.

She moved convulsively and backed into Brett's arms with a squeak of fear.

'Shh,' he murmured and flicked on the torch. 'It's only a kangaroo. I've been watching it for a bit. It's just curious. Kangaroos aren't renowned for attacking and eating people.'

'I k-know that,' Holly stammered. 'It must have been all the tales of Africa you told me. I feel terrible.' She added.

'What's wrong?' he queried with a hint of surprise.

'Stiff and sore. Everything's aching. How about you?'

'I'm too damn cold to feel a thing. Come closer,' he ordered, and as she turned around with difficulty he gathered her into his arms. 'It's all the result of bouncing around in the plane, performing heavy tasks and sleeping on a river bed.'

'I suppose so. Mmm…at least that's a bit warmer. Do you mind if I really burrow in?'

'Why should I mind?' He stroked her back. 'In the light of hypothermia, it's the only thing to do. Just relax if you can.' He pulled the thin blankets from the plane more securely over her.

She was too grateful to protest, and gradually the protection of both blankets plus his body brought her some warmth, and her aching muscles unknotted a little.

She wasn't aware of the moment things changed—the moment when it wasn't only warmth and comfort she was seeking, or receiving, but something different. It came about so subtly it seemed entirely natural, a natural progression towards a greater closeness that claimed them both at the same time.

His hands slipped beneath her clothes as their mouths touched and he teased her lips apart. She moved her hands and slid them beneath his windcheater, responding to his kiss as she hugged him. From then on she forgot the cold and the discomfort of the river bed; she was lost to all good sense, she was to think later.

But, at the time, it was magic. She remembered something he'd said to her at the masked ball about celebrating her lovely, slim body to both their satisfactions. It wasn't quite like that—they were too hampered by clothes, covers and freezing night-air for that—but he gave her an intimation of what it would be like if they were together on a bed, or anywhere smooth and soft.

He transported her mentally to an oasis of delight where her skin would feel like warm silk—as he'd also promised. Even in the rough environment of a dry river-bed he managed to ignite her senses to a fever pitch as he kissed and caressed her, as he touched her intimately and made her tremble with longing, need and rapture.

She had her own sensory perceptions. She drew her fingers through the rough dark hair on his chest; she laid her cheek then her lips on the smooth skin of his shoulder, before returning her mouth to his to be kissed deeply again. And again.

She cupped her hand down the side of his face; she moved against the hard planes of his body. She was provocative, pressing her breasts against him and tracing the long, strong muscles of his back.

She was alight with desire for Brett Wyndham, she thought, when she could think. Alight, moving like a warm silken flame he couldn't resist in his arms.

How much further things would have got out of hand between them, she was never to know as a belligerent bellow split the chilly air.

They both jumped convulsively then scrambled to their feet, rearranging their clothes as best they could as Brett also searched for the torch. When he found it, it was to illuminate a mob of wild-looking cattle, some with huge horns, advancing down the creek bed towards them.

'Bloody hell!' Brett swore. 'Stay behind me,' he ordered. He reached up and tore a spindly limb from a tree growing out of the bank. 'They're probably as surprised as we are.'

With threatening moves, and a lot of yelling and whistling, he dispersed the mob eventually—but only after they'd got uncomfortably close. Then they took to their heels as if of one mind and thundered back the way they'd come, causing a minor sandstorm and leaving them both coughing and spluttering, sweating and covered in sand.

'Just goes to show, you don't have to go to Africa for wildlife excitement,' he said wryly.

'You have quite a way with cattle!'

'That was more luck than anything.'

Holly frowned. 'They didn't look like Brahmans.'

'They weren't, that's why I was a bit lucky. They were cleanskins, in case you didn't notice.'

'Cleanskins?'

'Yes. Rogue cattle that have evaded mustering and branding and therefore are not trained to it. Independent thinkers, in other words. Throwbacks to earlier breeds.'

'Oh.'

'Yep.' He dragged a hand through his hair and put the torch on the ground. 'Where were we?'

CHAPTER SEVEN

THEY stared at each in the torchlight then started to laugh.

In fact, Holly almost cried, she laughed so hard; he put his arms around her.

'I know, I know, but one day I will make love to you with no interruptions,' he said into her hair.

Holly sobered and rested against him.

'Look,' he added. 'You can just see the horizon. A new day.'

'How long will it take them to come?' she asked.

'No idea, but just in case we have to spend another night we'll need to get organized.'

Holly sat up. 'Another night?'

'That's the worst-case scenario,' he said. 'The best is that they know we're missing and they know roughly the area. So they'll keep looking until they find us.'

But full daylight brought another challenge: rain and low cloud.

'I thought this was supposed to be the dry season,' Holly quipped as a shower swept up the river bed.

They'd moved all their gear under tree-cover on the bank as best they could as soon as the clouds had rolled

over. They were sitting under the cover of the plastic
V-sheet Brett had hooked up from some branches.

'It is. Doesn't mean to say we can't get the odd shower.
You know…' He stared out at the rain drumming down
on the river bed, then looked at her. 'If you cared to take
your clothes off, it might be quite refreshing.'

Holly looked startled. 'Do you mean skinny-dip?'

He shrugged. 'Why not? It's our only chance of getting clean for a while.'

Holly drew a deep breath and closed her eyes. 'Clean,'
she repeated with deep longing. Her eyes flew open and
she jumped up and started shedding clothes.

Brett blinked, not only at the fact that she did it but
at the speed she did it. A rueful little smile twisted
his lips as she stopped short at her underwear—a lacy
peach-pink bra with matching bikini briefs.

'That's as far as I'm going to go,' she told him, and
climbed down the bank to run out into the rain with
something like a war cry.

He had to laugh as he watched her prancing around
for a moment, then he stood up to shed his clothes down
to his boxer shorts and climbed down the bank to join
her.

It was a heavy, soaking shower but it didn't last that
long. As it petered out, Holly—now more subdued—said
in a heartfelt way as her wet hair clung to her head and
face, her body pale and sleek with moisture, 'That was
divine!'

She ran her hands up and down her arms and licked
the raindrops from her lips.

'Yes, although I didn't expect you to do this.' He

grinned down at her and flicked some strands of wet hair off her face.

'I suspect most girls would have done the same if they'd been through what we have. Now, if only I had a towel…'

As she spoke, thunder rumbled overhead and a fork of lightning appeared to spear into the river bed not far from them.

Holly jumped convulsively and flew into Brett's arms. He picked her up and carried her swiftly to their makeshift shelter.

'Th-that was so close,' she stammered.

'Mmm…I don't think it'll last long; it's just a freak storm.' But he held her very close as more thunder rumbled.

'Lightning,' she said huskily, 'Is right up there with flying foxes for me. It's funny; there are a whole heap of things I can be quite cool about.'

'Mexican bandits and sheikhs?'

'Yep—well, relatively cool. But lightning—' she shivered '—I don't like.'

'Just as well I'm here, then,' he murmured and bent his head to kiss her.

'This—this is terrible,' Holly gasped, many lovely minutes later.

'What's so terrible?' He drew his hands down her body and skimmed her hips beneath the elastic of her briefs.

They were lying together beneath the protection of the plastic sheet in each other's arms on one of the blankets. They were damp but not cold—definitely not cold…

'How did I get to the stage of not being able to keep my hands off you?'

He laughed softly. 'For the record, I'm in the same boat.'

'But it's been so *fast*. There's got to be so much we don't know about each other.'

'It's *how* you get to know people that matters.'

'Maybe,' she conceded. 'I guess it helps, but there's an awful lot I don't know about you.'

He opened his mouth, appeared to change his mind and then said, 'Such as?'

Holly went to sit up but he pulled her back into his arms.

'In fact, you know more about me than most people,' he growled into her ear.

'But, for example—' She hesitated suddenly aware that she was about to tread on sacred ground, from an interviewer's perspective. But surely she was more than that now? 'I know you were engaged and that it didn't work out, but I don't know why. And I sense some—I don't know—darkness.'

She felt him go still for a moment, then his arms fell away and he sat up and stared through the dripping view to the river bed.

Holly sat up too after a couple of minutes, during which he was quite silent.

'Have I offended you?' she ventured hesitantly. 'I didn't mean to.'

He turned his head and looked down at her. Her pink bra had a smudge of mud on it, but he could see the outline of her high, pointed breasts clearly. Her waist was tiny, tiny enough to span with his hands, but her hips were delicately curved and positively peachy.

He rubbed his jaw. 'No.' He smiled suddenly and ironically. 'Are you open to a suggestion?'

'What is it?' she asked uncertainly.

'That we put some clothes on? Just in case a rescuer arrives.'

Holly stared at him, convinced she'd crossed a forbidden barrier, then she looked down at herself and took a sharp little breath. She scrambled up. 'Definitely!'

The thunder storm moved away pretty quickly as Brett had predicted, and there was no more rain, but the low cloud-cover remained.

'That's got to make it harder for them to find us,' she said as they ate a very light lunch, with a view to preserving their limited supplies. They'd also rationed the water, but Brett had found some shallow rock pools with fresh water in them for future use.

By mid-afternoon the cloud cover had cleared and they heard two planes fly over—not directly overhead, but fairly close.

They said nothing during the tense wait both times, just exchanged wry little looks when the bush around them returned to silence.

Brett returned to the plane and, after crawling in with some difficulty, spent some time working on the radios but to no avail.

By four o'clock they were sitting back against their rock in the shade when he put his arm around her. Without any conscious thought, she leant her cheek against his shoulder.

'There is an option to consider now,' he said. 'We could walk out.'

'Is that a viable option?' she queried.

'It's not what I'd prefer to do. At least we're visible here—the plane is, anyway. I do have a rough idea of where we are, though, and where this river leads. But it's a long walk—maybe a couple of days.'

'What's at the end of it?'

'A cattle station near the head waters. We'd have to travel light, more or less food and water only. We'd really have to eke out the food, but it could be done.'

'What if someone spots the plane but we're not there?'

'We'd leave a note, but anyway they'd automatically assume we've followed the river bed. You see—' He paused and glanced at her, as if he wasn't quite sure whether to go on, then said, 'I didn't mention this yesterday but there's the possibility that none of our signals or radio calls were picked up. That means our position won't be known except very roughly, and we did make a detour.'

'Ah,' she said on a long-drawn-out breath. 'Well, then, I guess it makes sense to take things into our own hands. At least,' she added rather intensely, 'We'd be doing something!'

'My thoughts entirely.'

'And if we take the V-sheet with us we can always wave it if anyone flies overhead.'

'Good thinking,' he said, and kissed her on the top of her head. 'But listen, it could mean a very cold night. He sat up. 'Unless I make a sled of some kind so we could take a bit more with us—a blanket, at least. Come to that,' he said as if he was thinking aloud, 'once we're well away from the plane, we could make a fire. I had thought of doing that this afternoon, but well away from the plane.'

'Send up smoke signals, you mean?' she asked humorously.

'Something like that,' he replied with a grin. 'But everything's still damp. Tomorrow it may have dried out if we get no more rain. Uh, I have to warn you, though—this river bed could have rapids in it that would mean rock climbing, now its mostly dry, so it could be a very arduous walk.'

'And there could be wild cattle, there could be dingoes, heaven alone knows what,' she said with a delicious little shiver of anticipation of adventure.

His eyebrows shot up, then he laughed down at her. 'You're a real character—you're actually looking forward to it.'

'I was never one for sitting around! Perhaps we should have gone today,' she added seriously.

'No. It'll have done us the world of good to have a lay day after all the trauma of yesterday. But an early night'll be a good idea. Should we put it to the vote?'

'Aye aye, skipper—I vote yes.'

'OK. We'll get to work before the light runs out so we can leave at the crack of dawn tomorrow morning.'

It was just that, barely light, when they set off the next morning.

They'd finished all their preparations the afternoon before and spent a companionable night. Holly was at least buoyed up by the prospect of some action rather than sitting around waiting for what might not come. The more she thought about the vast, empty terrain surrounding them, the more she realized it could be like looking for a needle in a haystack.

Brett used the axe to make two long poles from tree branches and, using a variety of clothes, they constructed a light but sturdy sled for carrying stuff. Holly wrought two back-packs out of long-sleeved shirts.

Between them they smoothed an area of sand in the middle of the creek bed, helped by its dampness, and in big letters they wrote WALKED UPSTREAM, with several arrows pointing in the direction they would take. Then they lined the scores the letters had made in the sand with small rocks to make them more lasting and visible.

Brett also wrote a note and left it in the plane. He pointed out that the heavy shower of earlier had been a blessing for another reason, apart from allowing them to clean up a bit—it would also provide rock pools of fresh water along the way.

Not surprisingly—after a light supper of sardines on biscuits, and half a tube each of condensed milk for energy plus one cup of water each—they had little trouble falling asleep. Even the cold hadn't bothered Holly as much as it had the night before. Being curled up in Brett's arms gave her a lovely feeling of security.

She did wonder, briefly, where all the passion that had consumed them last night had gone, and concluded that either she had touched a nerve he hadn't wanted to be touched although he'd been perfectly normal during the day—or the physical exertion they'd expended had simply worn them out too much even to think of it.

She was to discover soon enough that being tired was no guard against anything...

It was a long, arduous day.

They walked in the cool of the morning, they slept beneath some leafy cover through the midday heat and they walked again in the afternoon.

It was fairly easy going, as far as sand could be easy, and they encountered no rocks they had to climb over.

They did see some pools of water and a couple of times they saw freshwater crocodiles slither into them.

She marvelled at Brett's strength and tirelessness as he towed the sled with a belt around his waist, as well as carrying a backpack.

As for herself, she sang songs to keep herself going when she would have loved to lie down and die. And she thought a lot as she trudged along, thoughts she'd never entertained before, about mortality and how, when you least expected it, swiftly, you could be snuffed out. It was delayed reaction to the plane crash, probably, but nonetheless to be taken seriously. It was about seizing the day or, instead of looking for perfection in every thing you undertook, letting the way life panned out have some say in the matter.

Brett took a lot of the credit for keeping her going. Every now and then he made her stop and he massaged her shoulders and back, or he told her jokes to make her laugh. He'd insisted on adding her backpack to the sled when she was battling.

Fortunately they both had hats in their luggage and Holly had a tube of factor thirty-plus sunscreen with which they'd liberally anointed themselves. This proved to be a mixed blessing, causing the sand to stick to them.

But there were some marvels to observe along the way: some black cockatoos with red tail feathers sailed overhead, with their signature lazy flight and far-away calls. They also saw a huge flock of pink-and-grey galahs and a family of rock wallabies.

Otherwise, the hot, still bush all around them was untenanted, even by wild cattle. Again they heard plane engines a couple of times but, the same as the day before, the planes were nowhere near enough to see them.

Then, just as they were about to call it a day, they got a wonderful surprise: the river bed wound round a corner and opened into a lagoon, a lovely body of water full of reeds, water lilies and bird life and edged with spiky, fruit-laden pandanus palms.

'Is it a mirage?' Holly gasped.

Brett took her hand. 'No, it's real.'

'Thank heavens! But is it full of crocodiles?'

'We'll see. Look.' He pointed. 'There's a little bay and a rock ledge with a beach above it. There's even a bit of a shelter. Good spot to spend the night.'

Holly burst into tears, but also into speech. 'These are tears of joy,' she wept, and laughed at the same time. 'This is just so—so beautiful!'

He hugged her. 'I know. I know. Incidentally, you've been fantastic.'

The shelter was rough-hewn out of logs, closed on three sides with a bark roof. There was evidence of occupation, a burnt ring of sand within a circle of rocks outside, and a couple of empty cans that had obviously been used to boil water over a fire.

'We can't be too far away from somewhere!' Holly enthused as she slipped her backpack off with a sigh of relief. Then she sat down, and took her boots off and wiggled her toes with another huge sigh, this time pure pleasure.

'No,' Brett agreed as he cast around, looking at the ground inside and outside the shelter. 'But there's no sign of— Ah, yes, there is.' He squatted down and outlined something in the sand with his fingers. 'A hoof print. Who ever uses this place comes by horse.'

'A horse, a horse, my kingdom for a horse!' Holly carolled. 'Or a camel. Or a donkey!'

Brett laughed.

'So who do you think uses it?' she enquired.

'A boundary rider—a mustering team, maybe.' He stood up. 'Whoever, we could be closer to the homestead than I thought.'

'That is music to my ears. Now, if only I wasn't covered in a repulsive mixture of sweat, sand and sunscreen, I'd be happy.'

'There's an easy remedy for that.' As he spoke Brett pulled off his shirt. 'I'm going for a swim.' He stripped off to his boxer shorts again and jogged down to the beach.

'But…' Holly temporized, thinking inevitably of crocodiles.

'This is fresh water,' he called back to her after he'd scooped a handful up and tasted it. 'And this,' he added as he waded in up to his waist, sending a variety of birds flying, 'is an old Aboriginal remedy for crocs.'

He started to beat the water with his palms. 'Frightens them off. Come in, Holly. I'm here anyway.'

She hesitated only a moment longer, then started shedding her clothes down to her underwear. Today she was wearing a denim-blue bra and matching briefs. She went into the water at a run in case her courage gave out to find it was divine, cool and refreshing, cleansing, incredibly therapeutic.

They played around in it for over half an hour then came out to the chilly air; it was close to sunset.

'Use whatever you can to dry off properly,' he recommended. 'We can always dry clothes tomorrow in the sun.' They'd only brought one change of clothes each.

'What if it rains again?'

'I doubt it will.' He towelled himself vigorously with a T-shirt and looked around. 'You know what they say— red sky at night, shepherd's delight.'

'Oh.' She looked around; the feathery clouds in the sky, a bit like a huge ostrich-feather fan or a group of foxtails, turned to orange as she watched.

'Anyway, I'm going to build a fire, so we can dry things beside it as well as keep warm. But get dressed and warm in the meantime.' He hung his shirt on a nail in the shelter wall and pulled on jeans and his second T-shirt. He was just about to turn away when he kicked his toe on something sharp protruding from the sandy floor.

He knelt down and, using his long fingers, unearthed a metal box. It wasn't locked, and what it contained made him say with absolute reverence, 'Holy mackerel! Look at this.'

Holly was now dressed in a pair of long cotton

trousers and her long-sleeved blue blouse. She bent down and looked over his shoulder. 'Oh my,' she breathed. 'Coffee! Tea! And a plate and a cup. I could kill for a cup of tea or coffee; don't mind which. But what's the other thing?' She frowned.

'This.' He lifted the red plastic spool out of the box. 'Is like gold. It's a fishing reel, complete with lure.' He showed her the curved silvery metal plate with a three-pronged hook on it. 'And sinker. I wondered if there'd be fish in the lagoon; there usually are.' He stood up. 'I was thinking I could kill for a beef steak, but a grilled fish would do nicely. All right, I'm going to collect firewood, you're going to fish.'

'Uno problemo—I have never used one of those things.'

'I'll show you how. Just watch.' He walked to the rocky ledge above the lagoon and unwound about a metre of the fishing line from the reel with the lure on the end. Holding the reel facing outward in one hand, he swung the lure on the line round several times then released it towards the water. The fishing line on the reel sang out as it followed suit, and she heard the lure plop into the water.

'Now what?' she asked keenly.

'Hold the line—you can put the reel down—and when you feel a tug on the line give it a jerk and pull the line in. Try.' He wound the line back onto the reel and handed it to her.

It took Holly several goes—the first time she hooked the lure into a tree—but finally she got it right and was left in charge in the last of the daylight as Brett went to collect firewood.

Her ecstatic shout when she felt the first tug on the line and pulled in a fish set all the water birds squawking in protest. Getting it off the line was her next test. Brett had to show her how to wrap one of her socks around the fish so she could hold it with one hand and wiggle the hook out of its mouth with the other. By the time he'd collected a big pile of wood and was setting the fire, she'd caught six very edible fish.

Brett had a go but caught none.

The first thing they did when the fire was going was boil water in one of the tins and make a cup of coffee, which they shared. Then, using a grid he'd found under one of the rocks around the fire area, Brett grilled the fish, which he'd cleaned with his penknife.

They shared the plate and ate the fish with their fingers.

'I don't know why,' Holly said, 'But this is the best fish I've ever tasted.'

'Could be a couple of reasons.' He glanced at her in the light of the blazing fire, but she didn't see the wicked little glint in his eye. 'After two days of ham and sardines on biscuits, anything would taste good.'

Holly pouted. 'That's one, what's the other?'

'I'm a good, inventive cook.'

'All you did was put them on a grid.'

'That's *not* all,' he countered. 'I had that part of the fire going to perfection so it wouldn't burn them, dry them out or leave them raw.'

'But I caught them!'

'So that makes them very superior fish?'

'Yes,' she said with hauteur, then giggled. 'You wouldn't be a little miffed because you *didn't* catch any?'

He looked offended. 'No. What makes you say that?'

She shrugged, still smiling. 'Just that I can't help feeling very proud of the achievement.' She paused and sobered. 'If I wasn't so worried about my mother, I'd really be enjoying all this.'

'We may be able to end her suspense sooner than we thought—end everyone's.'

'I hope so,' Holly said fervently. 'And she is an eternal optimist.'

She was sitting with her knees drawn up and her arms around them. He was stretched on the sand with his head on his elbow. Because of the fire they were not rugged up to the nines, and Holly had arranged the V sheet in the shelter for them to lie on, with the one blanket they'd brought covering them.

Brett thought to himself, as he watched her in her light trousers and blue shirt, with her bare feet and the fire gilding her riotous hair, that she had never looked more desirable.

Was it because she'd coped so well? he wondered. Had that added to his attraction to her? But was he going to be able to overcome her wariness? She might tell him she couldn't keep her hands off him, but he knew that deep down she was still wary, still burnt by her previous experience.

And he thought about *his* wariness—about the discovery he'd made about himself that he hated and feared, and made him wonder if he was a fit mate for any woman.

It was, of course, the thing Holly had sensed in him, the thing she couldn't put her finger on—the thing he had never wanted to admit to himself. But what was between them wasn't the same thing that had happened to him before, was it?

This was a powerful attraction, yes, but it was also affection. Yes, it was sweet, but it was also sane and sensible because she would fit into his lifestyle so completely...

Then he realized she was returning his regard, her deep-blue eyes very serious, as were the young, lovely curves of her face.

A slight frown came to his face, because he had no idea what she was thinking. Was she thinking about her mother? He got the feeling she was not.

'Holly?'

She looked around, as if unwilling for him to see what was in her eyes. She looked at the fire, at the darkened lagoon beyond, at the moon rising above them and the pale smoke of the fire wreathing against the dark blue of the sky. 'I think I'm running out of steam,' she said at last. 'I feel terribly weary.'

'I'm not surprised,' he said after a moment, and stood up. 'Come to bed. But have a cup of water first; I don't want you to dehydrate.'

'Are you coming to bed?' she asked.

'Shortly. I'm going to get more wood so we can keep the fire going as long as possible. Goodnight.' He held his hand out to her.

She took it and got to her feet. 'I— Thank you.'

'What for?'

'All you've done today, and tonight. The swim, the fish, the fire; that's all been magic.'

He frowned. 'You're not afraid we won't get out of this, are you?'

She shrugged. 'No. What will be, will be.'

He stared down at her intently for a moment then kissed her lightly. 'Sweet dreams, Holly Harding.' He turned away.

Holly woke from a deep, dreamless sleep at two o'clock. There was just enough light from the glowing embers of the fire for her to see her watch, but her movement woke Brett. She was resting in his arms.

'Sorry,' she whispered.

'Doesn't matter,' he mumbled.

It was nowhere near as cold as it had been the two previous nights, even though the fire had died down. The heat of it must be trapped within the shelter, she thought.

She went still as Brett pulled her closer into his arms and his mouth rested on her cheek. Her senses started to stir, started to clamour for his touch, for his kiss. But had he gone back to sleep?

Her lips parted and his mouth covered hers; no, he hadn't. But he hesitated, and Holly suddenly knew she couldn't bear it if he withdrew.

She put her hand on his cheek and arched her body against him, and found herself kissing his strong, tanned throat. He made a husky sound and then his hands moved on her body and she rejoiced inwardly, knowing they were claimed by the same need and desire.

Once again they fumbled with their clothes as best they could, but the rhythm of rapture made light work of it. She put her arms above her head and let his hands travel all the way down her, then gasped as they came back to her breasts.

She lay quietly, quivering in his arms, and allowed him to tantalize her almost unbearably as those fingers sought her most secret places. Then she wound her arms around him and kissed him as if her life depended on it.

He accepted the invitation to claim her completely in a way that brought them both intense and exquisite pleasure.

They were still moving to that pleasure as they slowly came back to earth, then they separated at last but stayed within each other's arms.

'We didn't say a word,' he murmured, and kissed her.

'It didn't seem necessary,' she answered. 'Did it?'

'No, but—' He broke off and lifted a hand to stroke her hair.

'I wanted to say something earlier,' she told him. 'When we were sitting by the fire—I wanted to say I didn't think I could do it.'

He raised his head and frowned down at her. 'Holly...'

'No.' She touched her fingers to his lips. 'Let me finish. I wanted to say I didn't think I could lie on this V-sheet without wanting to be held, kissed and made love to.'

He sat up abruptly.

'Not after everything,' she went on. 'Because you

were incredible—not only in all you did today, but in the way you kept me going.'

'Holly…'

She broke in again. 'I'm just happy to be with you tonight. It—it just seemed to be so fitting and right for the moment, and sometimes I think you need to *live* for the moment. But you don't have to worry about the future.'

He sank back beside her and pulled her into his arms again. 'I'm not worried about it. I'm looking forward to it. When will you marry me?'

CHAPTER EIGHT

HOLLY gasped, then evaded his arms and sat up urgently. 'That's exactly what I *don't* want you to feel you have to do!'

He propped his head on his elbow and looked up at her with a glint in his eyes she couldn't decipher. 'You've had time to work that out?' he queried.

She bit her lip. 'Obviously, otherwise it wouldn't have come to mind.'

He grimaced. 'But why not?' He lifted a hand and touched his fingers to her nipples.

Holly shivered but forced herself to concentrate. 'How could you suddenly want to marry me? I'm sure you don't ask every girl you sleep with to do that.'

He looked briefly amused. 'No. But it's not so sudden. It's been on my mind since you came to Haywire. Look, you asked me how I juggled things earlier: the truth is I'm at a bit of a crossroads. I'm getting tired of all the juggling I have to do. I'm thinking of coming home on a fairly permanent basis. That's what prompted the zoo idea—it's a way I can carry on my work and be here at the same time.'

Holly turned her head. 'Won't that be an awful wrench for you?'

'Sometimes,' he said slowly and pulled her back against him. 'And I'll probably always take off now and then; I won't be able to help myself. But it's time to put down some roots. The thing is—' He paused. 'I've had trouble really coming to grips with the idea—not the zoo, but putting down roots. Because I've had no-one to do it with. But now there's you.'

Holly tried to think. 'I'm—I don't know what to say. Please tell me, are you serious?'

'Deadly serious.'

She stirred against him. 'Brett, could I be—and I ask *this* seriously—a bit of a novelty for you?'

She felt him shrug. 'A wonderful novelty,' he agreed. 'But we also have a lot in common. You fitted into Haywire almost as if you'd been born to it.' He threaded his fingers through hers. 'Could you see yourself living there? Us living there?'

It occurred to Holly that she could. It was a lifestyle that encompassed all the things she loved: far away, exciting, different and still a challenge at times. And with a huge challenge coming up, if he went ahead with his plans for the zoo.

What about her career, though?

She could always freelance, she thought.

She even found herself contemplating a serious journalistic career focusing on the cause that was so dear to his heart and was becoming more and more fascinating to her.

Of course, there was the other factor: she was conscious of his body against hers and the sheer delight, the strength and warmth, it could bring her. Not only that, it was as if she'd found the centre of her universe in him.

She moved abruptly. 'I... Brett, could this not be love but something more—convenient?'

'It didn't feel convenient a little while ago. Did it for you?'

She shivered again as she relived their passion. 'No,' she whispered, shaken to her core.

'And there's this,' he went on very quietly. 'How easy would it be for you to get up and walk away from me?' He smiled ironically. 'Assuming it was possible anyway and we weren't marooned in an oasis in a bloody river-bed.'

She had to smile but it faded swiftly as she battled with how to answer him. 'I...' She stopped as tears suddenly beaded her lashes.

'Don't cry,' he said very quietly. 'It would be hell for me too.'

'The last thing I would want to feel is that you're sorry for me.' She sniffed.

'I'm not. But I do feel as if I want to look out for you.'

'That could be the same thing,' she objected.

'No. It means I care about you.'

Holly sniffed again. 'Do I have to make a decision right now?'

'Why not? We're never going to get as good an opportunity to think clearly.'

She frowned. 'What—how do you mean?'

'No outside influences at all.'

She swallowed in sudden fear. 'What if we don't get rescued or we don't find the station?'

His lips twisted. 'Perhaps the perfect solution. We could do a "me Tarzan, you Jane" routine. No, only joking. We will get rescued.' He pushed aside the layer of cover and took her in his arms. 'Believe me,' he added, and kissed her gently.

Holly felt herself melting within, and when he lifted his head she laid her cheek on his shoulder.

'Is that a yes?' he queried.

She hesitated. 'I don't know yet. I just don't know.'

He grimaced but said, 'Never mind. I'll ask you again every hour on the hour until our rescuers arrive or we arrive somewhere. Go back to sleep.' He looked at his watch over her head. 'We've got a couple of hours before dawn. Comfy?'

'Yes,' she breathed. 'Oh, yes.'

Five minutes later she was fast asleep, although Brett stayed awake for a while and contemplated this turn of events. Surely she wasn't planning to walk away from him now? he theorized.

It wasn't dawn that woke them; they slept well past it, in fact.

It was the sound of a man clearing his throat and saying, 'Excuse me, but were you two in a airplane crash?'

CHAPTER NINE

THEY both shot up. Holly immediately grabbed the blanket and pulled it up as she realized what a state of disarray she was in.

Not only was there a tanned, wiry little man with bowed legs and a big hat looking in on them, but two horses were looking over his shoulders with pricked ears and what appeared to be deep interest.

Even Brett was lost for words.

The man said, 'Don't mean to disturb anything, but if you are from the plane there's a hell of a hue and cry going on over you. Tell you what, I'll just take a little walk while you get—organized.' He wheeled his horses around and walked away.

Holly and Brett turned to each other simultaneously and went into each other's arms.

'I told you we'd get out of this,' he said as he hugged and kissed her.

'You did, you did!' she said ecstatically. 'And I offered my kingdom for a horse—I can't believe this! Where on earth did he come from?'

In the event, their saviour was a boundary rider for the station they were making for, and he was quite happy to wait while they had a swim. Fully clothed and decorous, they changed into their other set of clothing. He even made them a cup of coffee while he waited.

While they drank coffee, he explained how he'd heard the news of the loss of the plane just before setting out from the homestead on a routine inspection, and how he'd promised to keep his eyes open.

'Didn't see nothing, though,' he added. 'But last night I smelt smoke on the breeze and the breeze was coming from this direction, so I thought I'd take a look and see.'

'Is this your camp?' Brett asked.

'Sure is,' the man, Tommy, replied proudly. 'I put the shelter up, and they call it Tommy's Hut.'

'Well, your fishing gear was a lifesaver, Tommy. So was the rest of it. How far are we from the homestead?'

Tommy chewed a stalk of grass reflectively. 'Bout a three-hour ride, considering there's three of us and only two horses. Won't be able to make much time. You and the missus can share a horse.'

'Any family in residence at the homestead?' Brett enquired.

'Nope, just a manager. The place has gone up for sale, actually—family quarrels over money, I hear, so they need to cash it in. But they got radios and phones to get word out you're OK, and to rustle up a plane to get you back to Cairns.'

'Great.'

'Goodbye,' Holly said softly half an hour later when the camp had been tidied up and most of their gear stowed in the shelter.

She was perched in front of Brett on a tall brown horse.

'Talking to me?' he enquired.

'No. I'm farewelling a lovely spot, a place that was a bit of a lifesaver and a bit of a revelation.' She turned for a last look at the lagoon, the water lilies, the birds and the palms. 'An oasis.'

'Yes,' he agreed. 'And more.' But he didn't elaborate.

It was late that afternoon when they flew back into Cairns. A plane similar to the one they'd crashed in had retrieved them from the cattle station, where they'd taken fond farewells of their rescuer and his horses.

They hadn't had any time alone together at all.

What Holly hadn't expected, or even thought about, was that there would be an army of press waiting behind a barrier to greet them. She blinked somewhat dazedly into the flashlights as she stepped down onto the runway in the general-aviation section of the airport. Then she made out a face she knew in the crowd and, with a little cry, she ran forward and into her mother's arms.

A day later, Holly was still at Palm Cove.

Her mother had gone home and Holly had been in two minds as to whether she should go back to Brisbane too. She'd seen little of Brett, who'd been tied up with air-crash investigators and all sorts of authorities. She herself had kept a very low profile.

In fact, after she'd said farewell to her mother, she'd gone for a walk along the beach and felt like pinching herself. Had she dreamt that Brett Wyndham had asked her to marry him? Had she dreamt up a magic oasis that had become a place of even greater pleasure? No, she knew she hadn't dreamt that. She still had some marks on her body to prove it.

But was she a journalist with an interview to complete, or what?

'Remember me?'

She jumped as Brett ranged up alongside her. 'Oh. Hi! Yes, although I was wondering if I'd ever see you again.'

He took her hand and swung her to face him. He wore a loose, blue cotton shirt and khaki shorts; his feet were bare.

'I'm sorry.' He bent his head and kissed her lightly. 'Can you remind me the next time I'm tempted to crash-land a plane that the amount of paperwork involved is just not worth it? And it's not finished yet!'

Holly giggled. 'All right.'

'Incidentally, I sent a helicopter out to the crash site and Tommy's Hut. They brought all our stuff back.'

'Good. Although my mother brought me some clothes.' She looked down at the long floral skirt she wore with a lime T-shirt.

'Would she have brought anything appropriate for a ball?'

Holly stiffened.

'It's tonight,' he said. 'Please come as my partner. And to the wedding tomorrow evening.'

'No. Thank you, but no. I—'

'Holly, sit down. Look, there's a handy palm-tree here.'

'Brett' She tried to pull away, but he wouldn't let

her, and finally they sank down and leant back against the tree.

'You're looking a little dazed,' he said. 'And I can't blame you—'

'Yes, well, if I didn't dream it,' she interrupted, 'please don't ask me to marry you again, because at the moment I am— I don't know if I'm on my head or my heels.'

He stared down at her. 'You didn't dream it,' he said with a glimmer of a smile in his eyes. 'Although I won't ask—not immediately, anyway.' He sobered. 'But this ball is a way for us to be together tonight, because I can't get out of it and I'm having withdrawal symptoms. How about you?'

Holly drew her knees up, put her arms around them and rested her chin on them in a bid to hide the powerful tremor that had run through her.

'Holly?' He said her name very quietly.

She turned her head and laid her cheek on her knees. 'Yes. Yes, I am. I'm missing you.'

'Then?'

She sighed and looked out to sea. 'All right. Do you have to go off somewhere now?'

'Not for at least half an hour,' he said. 'What would you like to do?'

'In half an hour?' She smiled. 'Well, talk, I guess.'

He stretched out his legs as she sat up, and he put his arm around her. 'Did I tell you how fantastic you were?'

Holly made her preparations for the ball in a state of mind that could have been termed 'a quandary'.

On one hand, she wanted to be with Brett rather desperately but, on the other, did she want to be with him under the scrutiny of his family and doubtless a whole host of people?

Not only a host but probably a high-profile host.

It was in line with this thought that she followed an impulse and booked into a beauty parlour when she normally wouldn't have. The impulse was not only prompted by a need to hold her own in an upmarket throng; her nails were broken and ragged and her hair resembled a dry bird's-nest despite having washed it.

So she had a manicure and a deep-conditioning hair treatment, as well as a mini-facial. She came out of the parlour feeling a bit better about the ball and definitely better about her hair and nails.

Next decision was what to wear. For once in her life she was tempted to shop, then she remembered that her mother had brought one of her favourite dresses, one that was the essence of simplicity but which she always felt good in.

It was black, a simple long shift in a clinging silk jersey with a scoop neck and no sleeves. With it she wore a necklace made of many strands of fine black silk threaded with loops and whorls of seed pearls and tiny shells. It was the necklace that really made the dress, and the shoes. They were not strappy sandals but a pair of low court-shoes in silver patent with diagonal fine black stripes. Her mother had even packed the bag that went with the outfit, a small patent-leather purse that matched the shoes.

How had her mother known she would need these items? Holly wondered suddenly. Then she recalled with a smile that Sylvia never went anywhere without being fully prepared for any eventuality. It struck her suddenly—had her mother guessed that there was something between her only daughter and Brett Wyndham?

It probably was not such an unusual conclusion to come to since they'd been forced into each other's company for the last three days, not to mention the days that had gone before, and Sylvia could be pretty intuitive.

She shrugged and started to put on a light make-up.

Brett came to collect her from her room an hour early, and took her breath away in a dinner suit.

'You look lovely,' he said and took her hand.

'So do you,' she answered with a glint of mischief in her deep-blue eyes.

'Lovely?'

'In your own way.' She studied his tall figure in the beautifully tailored black suit. 'Distinguished. Dangerous.'

His eyebrows shot up 'Dangerous?'

'Dangerously attractive. Did I ever tell you that you were rather stunning as a Spanish nobleman?'

'No.' He grinned down at her. 'You were far too busy impersonating a French Holly Golightly and spinning me yarns about asses and camels.'

Holly gurgled with laughter. Somehow the ice was broken between them, which was to say, somehow she felt a lot better about going to this ball with him.

'I'm early,' he said as they walked away from her room, 'Because Sue is having pre-ball drinks in her suite. I'll be able to introduce you to her, as well as

Mark and Aria. Incidentally.' He paused. 'My ex-fiancée will be at the ball, and she could be at Sue's drinks. I don't think I told you she's in charge of all the wedding festivities.'

Holly missed a step.

He stopped beside her. 'She's a friend of Aria's, and she's the best at this kind of thing. It's been over between us for some time now.'

Nine months; it shot through Holly's mind. *It's not that long, is it?*

But she said nothing, although some of her feel-good mood about the ball ebbed a little as she thought of being confronted by Natasha Hewson.

She need not have worried, she soon discovered. Her presence both at Sue's drinks and the ball was that of a celebrity—the girl who'd survived the plane crash with Brett but kept a very low profile since.

Mark and Aria were warmly friendly, so was Sue Murray. And so was Natasha Hewson. She *was* the same redhead Holly had seen dining the night before they'd flown to Haywire.

She was also extremely beautiful, tall and exotic in a bouffant shocking-pink gown.

Holly did have a momentary vision of Natasha and Brett as a couple and thought they would have been absolutely eye-catching. But Natasha appeared to be happily in the tow of a handsome man, and Holly could detect no barely hidden undercurrents between her and Brett. Which was probably why what did eventuate later in the evening came as such a shock to Holly.

In the meantime, she started to enjoy herself.

The resort ballroom faced the beach and the cove

through wide glass windows, so the view was almost unimpeded. Due to a trick of the evening light, you felt as if you could lean across the cove and touch Double Island and its little brother.

Dinner was superb, a celebration of "reef and beef" that included the wonderful seafood found in the waters off the coast. Not only was dinner superb but the company beneath the chandeliers and around the exquisitely set tables was too.

Cooktown orchids decorated the tables, and the women's gowns, in contrast to the men in dark dinner-suits, brought almost every colour of the spectrum to the scene: primrose, topaz, camellia pink, sapphire, violet, oyster, claret and many more. Not only the colour, but there was every style and texture: there were silks, satins, taffetas, there were diaphanous voiles encrusted with sequins that flashed under the lights. There were skin-tight gowns, strapless ones, ruched and frilled ones. As it happened, there was only one plain-black one…

She and Brett dined at a table for eight that included his sister Sue as well as the bridal couple, Mark and Aria. Natasha Hewson was on the other side of the room.

After dinner, Brett invited her to dance.

'You know,' he said as she moved into his arms, 'You've done it again.'

She shot a startled look at him.

'You stole the show as Holly Golightly; you've done it here.'

Holly blinked, then shook her head. 'Oh, no.'

'Believe me, yes.' He pulled her close. 'Do you dance as well as you do everything else, Miss Golightly?'

She lowered her voice a notch. 'Possibly better than I ride, monsieur.'

He laughed and dropped a kiss on her hair.

Neither of them noticed that Natasha Hewson was watching them as Brett swung Holly extravagantly to the music. When they came back together, lightly and expertly, they danced in silence for a few minutes.

They really were well matched, but it wasn't only a rhythmic experience, Holly thought. It was a sensuous one too. She was aware not only of her steps but that she felt slim, vital and willowy.

As his dark gaze ran down her body, a frisson ran through her because she knew he was visualizing her breasts and hips beneath the black material. Nor could she help the same thing happening to her, being aware of his grace and strength beneath his dinner suit.

But as the moment threatened to engulf her in more specific fantasizing, the music came to an end. They came together but he didn't lead her off the floor.

He said instead with his arms loosely around her, no sign of humour in his dark eyes, 'Have you made up your mind, Holly?'

She took a breath. 'I— Brett, this isn't the time or place—'

'All right.' He broke in and took her hand. 'Let's do something about that.' And he led her off the floor, through a set of glass doors, out onto the lawn and behind a row of trees. There was no-one around. 'How about this?'

She took a frustrated little breath. Not only was there no-one for them to see, there was no-one to see them. 'Brett.' She paused, then took hold. 'All right, I've been thinking really seriously about it. It seems to make good sense.'

'There has to be more to it than that now.'

'Well, yes,' she conceded. 'I don't know how reliable that is, though.' She paused, then she said urgently, 'Please, could you give me a little longer? It's a huge step for me…' She trailed off a little desperately.

He said after a long moment, 'Only if I'm allowed to do this?' He took her into his arms.

'Do what?' she breathed.

'Kiss you.'

'Well…'

But he did the deed anyway. As she stood in the protective circle of his arms afterwards, she was trembling with desire and conscious of the need to say *yes, I'll marry you, I'll marry you…*

Some tiny molecule of resistance held her back. Something along the lines of *he always gets his own way* managed to slip above her other feelings. 'Will you?' she whispered. 'Give me a little more time?'

Something she couldn't decipher passed through his eyes, then his lips twisted. 'All right. So long as you stay by my side. The wedding's tomorrow evening—will you come?'

Holly hesitated.

'Or do I have to make all the concessions?' he asked rather dryly.

Holly shook her head. 'I'll come. But in the meantime perhaps we should get back in case people imagine all sorts of things?'

'Such as, I've made off with you and seduced you?'

He looked briefly amused. 'If it wasn't for Mark and Aria that's just what I'd like to do.'

Holly gazed at him and thought for a moment that, despite his dinner suit, he looked dark and pirate-like and quite capable of spiriting her off to a place of seduction. She shivered slightly.

'Cold?' He looked surprised.

'No. But I do need to visit the bathroom. I don't want to look...' She stopped.

'Thoroughly kissed,' he suggested with a definitely pirate-like smile. 'Believe me, it suits you.'

He took her hand and led her back inside.

Holly went to find the facilities. The only person she encountered as she crossed the foyer, other than staff, was Natasha Hewson in her beautiful bouffant shocking-pink gown that should have clashed with her hair but didn't. They stopped, facing each other.

'The bathroom is that a-way,' Natasha said, indicating the direction she'd come from.

'Thank you,' Holly replied, then paused a little helplessly.

'Do you think you'll hold him?' Natasha asked. 'Do you think you'll be the one he'll give up his jungles and his endangered species for? Or were you planning to join him? Don't,' she warned, 'be fooled by *this* Brett Wyndham.'

Holly couldn't help herself. 'What do you mean?'

'Not many of us are immune from that charisma—the good company, the man who makes you tremble, makes you laugh and want to die for him. But he's really a loner. He reminds me of one of the tigers he's trying to save: secretive, thrives on isolation and challenges, clever, dangerous.'

Holly blinked several times. 'Natasha,' she said then, 'Do you have any hopes of getting him back?'

Natasha Hewson shrugged her sleek, bare, beautiful shoulders. 'One day he'll realize that even tigers need a tigress. And that will be *me*.' She blew Holly an insolent kiss as she walked past her.

Fortunately, Holly found herself alone in the bathroom. Fortunately, because as she stared at herself in the mirror she could see how shell shocked she looked as she rinsed her hands.

It was printed in her eyes; it came from the fact that, whether wittingly or not, Natasha had pinpointed the core of her concerns about Brett.

Was he a loner who would never change? He himself had told her he'd probably always take off for the call of the wild. Would she ever get to know what that darkness she sensed in him was about? Would she be a convenient, handy wife who would give him roots, a family perhaps, but never be a soul mate?

She took a painful breath; that wasn't the only cause of her shell shock, intensely disturbing as it was. No, there was also the fact that it wasn't over between Brett and Natasha—it certainly wasn't over for Natasha—and that brought back terrible memories for Holly. Memories of being stalked by a bitter woman pushed almost over the edge.

I can't do it, she thought, and felt suddenly panic-stricken. *I have to get away—but how?*

She finally gathered enough composure to leave the

bathroom to find Brett waiting for her in the foyer. A rather grim, serious-looking Brett.

'Holly,' he said immediately. 'I've just had a call redirected to my phone because they couldn't raise you. Your mother—' he hesitated '—has been taken to hospital. She's going to be all right; it could be an angina attack, but they feel they have it under control. She's asking for you.' He put his arms around her. 'I'm sorry.'

'Oh!' Holly's eyes dilated. 'I've got to get down to her. Oh, it's late—there may not be flights. What will I do?' She stared up at him, agonized.

'Relax. It's all organized?'

'Organized? How?'

'The company jet is here in Cairns on standby. It's picking up some special wedding-guests in Brisbane tomorrow. It was due to fly out early tomorrow morning, but there's no reason for it not to leave now.'

'Thank you,' Holly breathed. 'I don't know how to thank you enough.'

'You don't have to. Look, I'd come with you—'

'No,' she interrupted. 'It's the wedding tomorrow. You need to be here for them.'

'I'll be down the day after. Promise me one thing.' He cupped her face. 'Don't go away from me, Holly Harding.'

She made a gesture to indicate that she wouldn't, but she did.

She wrote him a note while she was winging her way through the dark sky back to Brisbane and her mother. She told him she believed she'd never get to know him well enough to marry him. She told him she'd come to know that Natasha hadn't got over him, and maybe never would, and how that would always make her feel uneasy.

She bit the end of her pen and wondered how to point out that, if things hadn't been resolved completely for Natasha, perhaps they hadn't been for him either. But she decided against it. She asked him to please not seek her out because she wouldn't be changing her mind.

Then she wondered how to end her note so he wouldn't guess that her heart was breaking. Finally she wrote, *thanks for some wonderful experiences, and so long! It's been good to know you…*

She sealed it in an envelope and asked the stewardess to make sure it was delivered to Brett when the plane returned to Cairns.

Then she sat with tears rolling down her cheeks, feeling colder and lonelier than she'd ever felt in her life. How could she have grown so close to him in such a short time? she wondered. It was as if he'd taken centre-stage in her life and she had no idea how to go on with that lynchpin removed.

But it wouldn't have worked, she told herself; it couldn't have worked.

CHAPTER TEN

SEVERAL weeks later, Holly brushed another set of tears from her cheeks and wondered when she'd stop crying whenever she thought of Brett Wyndham.

What brought him to mind this early morning was the fact that she was walking down a beach on North Stradbroke island when she came across a fisherman casting into the surf.

North Stradbroke, along with South Stradbroke and Moreton islands, formed a protective barrier that created Moreton Bay. On the other side of the bay lay the waterside suburbs of Brisbane and the mouth of the Brisbane River. It was a big bay littered with sandbanks and studded with islands, and huge container ships threaded their way through the marked channels to the port of Brisbane. Holly was on the ocean side of North Stradbroke, affectionately known as 'Straddie' to the locals, where the surf pounded the beaches and where there was always salty spray in the air, and the call of seagulls. It was where her mother owned a holiday house, at Point Lookout.

Sylvia had recovered from what had turned out to be a chest infection rather than angina.

Holly had been coming to Point Lookout ever since

she could remember for school holidays, long weekends and annual vacations. Her father had loved it. The house was perched on a hillside with wonderful views of the ocean, Flat Rock and Moreton Island across the narrow South Passage bar.

She'd come over on the vehicle ferry in her car and some mornings she drove back to Dunwich on the bay side of the island. She had a fondness for Dunwich and for a particular coffee shop that served marvellous cakes and pastries, as well as selling fruit and vegetables.

There was also a second-hand shop, an Aladdin's cave of room after room of 'tat,' from jewellery to clothes, china to books and everything in between. Outside there were bird baths, garden gnomes and logs of treated woods. You could lose yourself for hours in it.

She loved wandering through the Dunwich cemetery, beneath huge old tress with the thick turf beneath her feet, reading the inscriptions on the graves that went back to the first settlers to come to Brisbane in the eighteen hundreds. She loved wandering down to the One Mile Anchorage where the passenger ferries came in and all sorts of boats rode at anchor.

Point Lookout might be upmarket these days, but Dunwich was actually an old mining town—although the only evidence of that was the huge trucks that rumbled through the little town laden with mineral sands mined on uninhabited parts of the island.

This overcast, chilly morning she'd decided not to drive across the island but take herself for a long, long walk along the beach. Her thoughts had been preoccupied with how she'd managed to persuade her mother that she needed some time on her own, although Sylvia rang her daily.

Of course, the reason she'd declared a need for peace and privacy and an inspirational setting was so she could write the Brett Wyndham interview.

Although she herself had heard nothing from Brett, to her amazement her editor Glenn had let her know that he'd been in touch and had given the go-ahead for her to write the piece, although he would still have the final say.

Why had he done that? she'd asked herself a hundred times. She could only assume he'd decided not to go back on his word in the interests of her career.

The magazine had given her two weeks' leave after the plane crash and she'd tacked on to that the two weeks' leave she was overdue. She had a week to go before she was due back at work, but she hadn't written a word. A fog seemed to descend on her brain every time she thought about it. She'd spoken to Glenn and explained the difficulty she was having.

'So if you're holding a slot for it, Glenn, I may not be able to reach the deadline—I'm sorry.'

'Holly.' Glenn had said down the line to her. 'You don't walk away from a plane crash and three days of wondering if you're going to survive without some mental repercussions. Don't force it; I'm not holding any slot for it. If it comes, when it comes, we'll see.'

Holly had opened her mouth to ask him if he'd heard from Brett again, but she'd shut it resolutely. Brett Wyndham needed to be a closed book for her now, but she'd clicked her tongue exasperatedly as soon as the thought had crossed her mind. How could he be a closed book when she had this interview to write?

Why hadn't she just admitted to Glenn she couldn't do it? Perhaps she could hand her notes to someone else—but so much of it was still in her head...

On the other hand, why couldn't she grit her teeth and get herself over him?

You did it once before, she reminded herself. *Yes, but I came to hate and despise* that *person,* she answered herself. *I could never hate Brett...*

If she'd had any doubts about that, they were quashed as she walked down the beach and saw a man fishing. She stopped to watch. She saw the tug on his line and the way he jerked the rod back to set the hook in the fish's mouth, just as Brett had shown her, although she'd only had a reel. She watched him wind the line in and saw the silver tailor with a forked tail on the end of it.

She took a distressed breath and turned away as she was transported back to the lagoon in the savannah country, with its reeds, water lilies and all its birds, where she'd swum and caught fish; where she'd sat over a fire; where she and Brett Wyndham had made love without saying a word.

Wave after wave of desolation crashed through her like the surf on the beach as she acknowledged what she'd been trying to deny to herself: that he would always be with her. He would always be on the back roads of her mind. There would always be a part of her that would be cold and lonely without him.

How it had happened to her in such a short time, she still didn't fully understand. She knew there were things about him she didn't know, areas perhaps no-one, no woman, would ever know. But it changed not one whit the fact that she loved him.

She knew that somehow he'd helped her overcome her fear of men and relationships. And she knew something else—that it wasn't her old fears that had affected her so badly that evening at Palm Cove when confronted by Natasha, it was her dreadful sense of loss because she'd come to know that it could never work for them.

She didn't notice that it had started to rain and that the fisherman had packed up and gone home after glancing uncertainly in her direction a couple of times. She ignored the fact that she was soaking wet, so consumed was she by a sea of sadness.

Then, at last, she turned towards the road and started to trudge home.

There was a strange car parked outside the house.

Well, not so strange, she realized as her eyes widened. It was a car she'd actually driven—a silver BMW X5—and as she came to a dead stop Brett got out of it. Brett, looking impossibly tall in charcoal jeans and a black rain-jacket.

They simply stared at each other, then he cleared his throat. 'Holly, you're soaked. Can we go in?'

She came to life, reached into her pocket for her key then stopped. 'Why… Why have you come?'

'I need to talk to you. You didn't think I'd leave it all up in the air like that, did you?'

'I don't think there's any more to say.'

'Yes, there is.' He closed the gap between them and took the key from her. 'And you need to get warm and dry before you get pneumonia. What have you been doing?'

'Walking. Just walking.'

He took her hand and propelled her down the path to the front door, where he fitted the key and opened the door. With gentle pressure on her shoulders, he manoeuvred her inside.

The front door opened straight into an open-plan living, dining and kitchen area. The floors were polished boards, the furnishings comfortable but kept to a minimum. The view was spectacular even on a day like today as showers scudded across the land and seascapes.

'Holly.' He turned her round to face him. 'Holly, go and have a shower. I'll make us a hot drink in the meantime.'

She licked her lips.

He frowned. 'Are you all right?'

She swallowed and made a huge effort to recover from the shell shock of his presence. 'Yes. Fine. Oh.' She looked down at herself. 'I'm dripping! I'll go.' And she fled away from him towards the bedroom end of the house.

He followed her progress with another frown, then turned away and walked into the kitchen area.

Twenty-minutes later Holly reappeared, wearing a silky dressing gown tied at the waist.

She'd hastily dried her hair and, because it looked extremely wild, she'd woven it into a thick, loose plait.

'I hope you don't have anything against plaits,' she said brightly as she reappeared. 'There was *nothing* else to do with it. Ah.' She looked at the steaming mugs on the kitchen counter and inhaled. 'Coffee. Thank you.

Just what I need. Do bring yours into the lounge; we might as well be comfortable.' She took her mug over to an armchair.

He followed suit and sat down opposite. 'You seem to have made a bit of a recovery.'

She grimaced. 'I wasn't expecting you, although I had been thinking of you. I guess I got a bit of a surprise. How did you find me?'

'I persuaded your mother to tell me where you were.'

Holly's lips parted in surprise, which he noted with a faint, dry little smile.

Holly sat back. 'I'm surprised she didn't ring me.'

'You have been out for quite a while,' he pointed out.

Holly sipped some coffee. 'So, why have you come?' she asked quietly. 'You don't have to explain to me why you've gone back to Natasha. I understand.'

'I haven't.'

'Then you should.'

'No.' He put his mug down on a side table. 'And I need to tell you why.'

'Shouldn't you be telling her?'

'I have. Holly, will you just listen to me?' he said with a bleak sort of weariness that was quite uncharacteristic.

'Sorry,' she said on a breath of surprise. 'I'm sorry.'

He beat a little tattoo on the arm of his chair with his fingers. 'This is not generally known outside the family, but my father had a very violent temper.'

Her lips parted. 'I wondered—I mean, I sensed

there was something about your father...' She couldn't go on.

'You were right. I hated him. I hit him once when he and my mother were arguing. She, and I, were usually the ones he took his temper out on. I can't say she was blameless.' He stopped and sighed. 'She should have got out, but it was as if there was this life-long feud going on between them that neither of them could let go of.'

'Why you, though?' Holly whispered. 'I mean you, as opposed to your brother and sister?'

He shrugged. 'Oldest son—maybe he saw me as a threat. I don't know. I do know he never stopped putting me down and I swore that when I took over I would never look back.

'I haven't. Things are in far better shape than they ever were when he was at the helm. But I guess I have to credit him with my interest in animals.'

Holly blinked. 'How so?'

'It was a world I could retreat into when things got impossible—my dogs, my horse and more and more anything on four legs. But the real irony is, much as I hated him, I'm not so unlike him.'

Holly stared at him, struck speechless.

'I also have a temper at times. I also got into a relationship that was—explosive.'

'Natasha,' Holly breathed, her eyes huge.

He nodded and rubbed his jaw. 'Once the first gloss wore off, we argued over the little things, we fought over the big things. We drove each other crazy, but she didn't see it that way. Every grand reunion we had seemed to reassure her that while it might be tempestuous between us—perhaps that even added a little spice to it for her—it was going to endure.

'I don't think she had any idea that I was really alarmed at the way I felt at times. I couldn't tell her. I couldn't put it into words, but I knew I had to get out. Whereas she thought that the fact we were so good in bed was going to compensate for the rest of it. But I could see myself looking down a tunnel at something that closely resembled my parents' marriage.'

'So—so you walked away?'

'Yes, I walked away. I broke it off. I told her— All I told her was that I wasn't cut out for marriage; I was a loner.' He shook his head. 'It was what I preferred to believe rather than admit the truth to myself. I hated the thought that there was any way I could resemble my father. Now, looking back, I can see it was always there. That's why I prided myself on being on the outside in my affairs with women, never deeply, crucially involved. Until Nat managed to break through.'

Holly put a hand to her mouth. 'Have you told her now?'

'Yes.'

'What happened?'

'She didn't believe me at first, but I had some other insights that I tried to explain. Such as—' he paused '—how egos get involved in these matters. How we were two naturally competitive people with a penchant for getting our own way, and we always would be. But that real hole in the gut and the heart, that sense of loss for someone who is not there for you, hadn't touched us. Not that kind of love.'

He got up and walked over to the windows.

Holly stared at his back and the lines of tension in his body.

'She understood that?' she queried huskily.

'I don't know. It made her stop and think. But it clarified things for me. We were never right for each other.' He said it sombrely but intensely.

'How can you be sure?'

He turned at last. 'Because that hole in the gut and heart slammed into me when I got your note.'

Holly's mouth fell open.

'That sense of loss and love almost crippled me, because I knew you were right to go away from me.'

'Brett,' Holly whispered. 'In light of all this, and the fact that you did ask me to marry you...'

'Let me finish,' he broke in. 'I asked you to marry me out of respect, affection, admiration—the way you seemed to fit into my life. But I told myself it wasn't a grand passion. I told myself I was safe from that, *you* were safe from that. Now I know I was wrong.

'I feel more passionate about you than I've ever felt in my life. It wasn't until you left I realized I'd got my grand passions mixed up. But the problem is that whilst how we are—you and I—is different from anything that went before, I keep wondering if my father will come out somehow and that scares me. Scares me far more than it did with Nat.'

She found it hard to speak as her heart beat heavily somewhere up near her throat. 'What—what are you saying?' she asked jaggedly.

His shoulders slumped and he took an uneven breath. Then he said harshly, 'It's best if we say goodbye now, but I had to explain.'

Holly stumbled to her feet with her thoughts flying in all directions. Then, out of nowhere, her epiphany from the plane crash came back to her: her conviction that she should really put her past behind her and live for the future. Plus the belief that had come to her this morning—that this man meant more than anything in the world to her.

She clenched her fists. 'Brett, she *was* the wrong one for you. Just as your parents were probably wrong for each other. But you've dug into your psyche and exposed the roots of it all—that means you *can* cope with it. It also means you could never be a carbon copy of your father. Anyway, you aren't. I know.'

'Holly.' He walked over to her and touched his fingers lightly to her face. 'You're very sweet, but you don't know what can happen—although you should have an inkling of it. I did lose my temper with you once, and frightened you into the bargain.'

Holly looked backwards in her mind's eye and shrugged. 'It wasn't at me, in the first place. It was at some driver who got his licence out of a cornflake packet. And you made amends almost immediately. Right from then you've always protected me,' she said tremulously.

He looked away from her and a nerve beat in his jaw.

'And there's something I do know,' she continued barely audibly. 'I'd trust you with my life, Brett Wyndham. I believe in you with all my heart. You can walk away from me now, but I'll always believe in you, and I'll always carry you in my heart.' Tears slid down her cheeks but she didn't notice them.

He hesitated, then brushed her cheeks with his thumbs. 'It'll go; it'll pass.'

'No, it won't.'

'We haven't known each other that long.'

'That was my line,' she said huskily, and smiled faintly through her tears. 'Yours was, "it's how you get to know people that matters".'

'Holly,' he said on a tortured breath, then swept her into his arms.   He held her closely, not speaking, and little by little she began to feel the terrible tension in him receding. He said, 'I had to warn you.'

'I'm glad you did because I always knew there was something buried really deep within you that I didn't understand. Now we both know we can cope with it together.' She hesitated. Although it was no longer a primary concern for her, she had some sympathy and had to ask the question: 'How is Natasha?'

'She's decided to open a branch of her agency in London. She told me it was over for her, whatever the rights and the wrongs of it were.' He smiled slightly. 'Whatever else, she's not one to wallow.'

Holly rested against him and sniffed.

He tilted her chin so he could look into her eyes. 'Tears? For Nat?' he queried.

Holly considered denying it, but found she couldn't. 'I've held some not altogether complimentary opinions of Natasha Hewson,' she confessed. 'But I'd like to wish her well.'

'Me too,' he murmured. 'You know, you don't have to worry about her—in any other context.'

Holly nodded. 'I've got over that. It was silly to go

through life waiting for it to happen again. Anyway, compared to losing you, it just seemed to fade away.'

'Do you really mean that?'

She looked deep into his eyes and breathed. 'Yes.'

'Sure?' A glint of humour suddenly lurked in his dark eyes and she felt her heart starting to beat faster.

'Yes. Why?'

'You were the one who accused me of being thoroughly bad-minded. Like a leopard,' he added for complete clarification.

'Ah.' She controlled the smile that wanted to curve her lips. 'You were the one who kept making verbal passes at me, not to mention mentally undressing me in the most awkward circumstances!'

'In that respect, I have to warn you I'm unlikely to change my spots—and definitely not in the immediate future,' he told her gravely.

She relented and laughed softly. 'I actually like the sound of that. And there's something I can bring to it that'll be unique for us.'

He raised his eyebrows questioningly.

'A bed.' Her eyes danced. 'A real bed. Not a river bed. No sand, no plastic V-sheet or cardboard bedding, no wild cattle to frighten the life out of me…'

He stopped her quite simply by kissing her. Then he lifted his head and looked into her eyes. 'Since you were the one to bring it up, could you lead me to it before I expire with desire?'

She took his hand. 'Come.'

It was not only a bed, it was a double bed, with a beautiful silk coverlet in the colours of the sea and sky on a clear day. Beneath the cover, the linen was starched and white.

'This is almost too much luxury,' he remarked as he pulled the cover down and laid her on the sheets.

'I know. Despite the sand and everything, I have some wonderful memories of a certain lagoon and Tommy's Hut, as well as—'

'I bought it,' he interrupted.

'As well as— You *what*?' Holly sat up, wide-eyed and incredulous.

'I bought the station.'

'Brett,' she breathed. 'Why?'

'Why do you think?' He looked down at her. 'Because of its memories of us, and you.'

'I— I...' There were tears in her eyes as she slipped her arms around his neck. 'I had no idea you were so romantic.'

'Neither did I. Would you like it as a wedding present?'

'I—I'm speechless. Are you serious?'

He nodded and kissed her. He laid her back against the sheets again and leant over her. 'We can go back on our anniversaries.'

'That would be lovely; thank you,' she whispered. 'Oh, Brett, I don't know what more to say.'

He smiled into her eyes and started to unzip her track-suit top. 'We don't have to say anything. I seem to recall it working pretty well for us like that.'

'So do I. OK; my lips are sealed...'

But of course they weren't, as he took his time about undressing her. Then, when they were naked and celebrating each other's bodies, he took her to the edge several times, only to retreat and sculpt her breasts and hips with his lips and hands. She had to open her lips, not only to kiss him and his body, but to tell him that—much as she'd loved their love-making in Tommy's Hut—the freedom from clothes and the comfort they were experiencing now were adding a dimension to it that was mind-blowing; it drew a joyous response from her.

She moved in a way that obviously tantalized him. She grew bolder and touched him in a way that drew a growling little response from him.

Desire snaked through her from head to toe, but at times she felt as light as air and more wonderful than she'd ever felt in her life.

Then the rhythm changed and what he did to her was so intense, she was wracked with pleasure and begging for the only release she wanted.

'Now?' he breathed.

'Please, now,' she gasped, and they moved on together as one until he brought her to the shuddering peak of sensation he shared.

She was breathless and speechless as those waves of climax subsided slowly and they clung to each other. Finally they were still and he loosened his arms around her.

She took his hand and put it against her cheek. 'I love you,' she said huskily.

'I love you,' he answered. 'I always will.'

Later, when they were snuggled up together on the sofa sipping champagne and watching the afternoon sky clear up, she said rather ruefully, 'How is my mother? Did you see her or speak to her on the phone?'

'I went to see her. We have one thing in common, your mother and I.'

'What's that?'

'We'd both probably die for you.'

'You don't have to do that, either of you.' Holly wiped a couple of tears from her eyes. 'Just be friends.'

'We will. If you can convince her you're happy. You see, she told me that, if I hurt you again, I'd have her to contend with.'

Holly gasped. 'I didn't know she knew. She never said a word.'

'I actually always admired your mother,' he informed her.

Holly chuckled, then was struck by a thought. 'How did the wedding go?' she asked.

'The wedding was very nice—had I been in the mood to appreciate it.' He looked rueful.

'You...?' She hesitated.

'I felt like cutting my throat.' He played with a strand of her hair. 'But there was a positive note. Sue met someone at the wedding. She's very taken with him, and I get the feeling he could be the right one for her. Uh, talking of weddings...?'

'Yes. Let's,' Holly said contentedly, but hid the sudden sparkle of mischief in her eyes. 'I'm not into balls and barbecues, but I did think perhaps we could hire an island in the South Pacific? We'd need one with accommodation for, say, at least a hundred guests—and we could have fire walkers and luaus—'

'There's not much difference,' he broke in ominously, 'Between a beach barbecue and a luau.'

'Well, there is. Roast suckling-pigs on spits. We could all wear leis and dance those fabulous Polynesian dances to drums.'

'Holly, stop!' he commanded.

But she'd stopped anyway, because she couldn't stop laughing. 'If you could see your face,' she teased. 'Look, I'd be happy to marry you in a mud hut with a herd of giraffe as guests.'

He kissed her. 'You're a witch, you know. But we won't go to those lengths. Something small and simple?'

'Done! When?'

'A month from today?'

She looked at him innocently. 'Why do we have to wait so long?'

'Just in case you want to change your mind.'

'Brett.' All laughter fled. 'I won't,' she promised. 'I won't.'

'Darling,' Sylvia said a month later, 'Are you very sure about this?'

'Mum.' Holly put her bouquet down and pulled her mother to sit down beside her on her bed.

Sylvia looked beautiful in a cornflower-blue silk suit with a cartwheel hat and lilies of the valley pinned to her bodice.

Holly, on the other hand, was all in white, an exqui-site lace dress over a taffeta slip with a heart-shaped bodice, long-sleeves and slim skirt.

Her hair was loose, although suggestions had been

made that it should be put up or pulled back—suggestions she declined with a secret little smile in her eyes.

Her full veil fell from a sparkling coronet and her bouquet was made up of six just-unfurled roses, each a different subtle colour from cream through to salmon.

'Mum,' she said again. 'I know you're—I know you've got reservations about Brett. But you did send him to me because, you told me, you thought only I could decide what to do.'

'I know. And I did think that; I still do.' Sylvia heaved a sigh. 'It's just that sometimes people don't change, however much they want to.'

'That was what Brett was afraid of,' Holly said quietly. 'And he may never have, if he didn't have someone who really believed in him as I do. And you know what Dad always used to say?' Holly went on. 'If you really believe in something, you have to go for it, otherwise you're denying that belief.'

'That's true. Well, my darling, I hope you'll be as happy as I was with your father, even though we were like chalk and cheese,' Sylvia said.

They both laughed. 'I will, I will.' Holly kissed her mother.

The wedding was small but very beautiful.

The homestead without walls at Haywire was decorated with greenery and magnificent flowers, all flown in that morning along with the bouquets.

A small altar had been contrived at the library desk, where Holly had made notes on her first visit to Haywire, and a red carpet led to it.

A feast was laid out on tables covered in heirloom damask cloths that Sue had inherited from her grandmother; each table was decorated with orchids in silver pots.

Mark and Aria were there, looking bronzed and exuberant after their prolonged and exotic honeymoon. Sue Murray was there with her new man, looking like a new person.

Glenn Shepherd was there, quite resigned to the fact that he'd lost the Brett Wyndham interview, as well as his travel writer extraordinaire, although the magazine would be the first to break the news of the zoo. He and Holly had also discussed the possibility of her freelancing for the magazine.

Sarah was still in residence, so she was there as well as well as Kane, the station foreman, and some of the staff from the other stations. And there were friends of both Holly and Brett as well as Sylvia, of course.

Even Bella had been invited, and she wore a silver horseshoe attached to her collar.

There was a covey of small planes on the airstrip and they'd stay there for the night.

The ceremony itself was short but moving—mainly, as many noted after the event, because of the palpable emotion between the bride and groom.

They all sat down to the luncheon; the champagne flowed, and it moved on to become a party.

In fact the only ones to leave were Brett and Holly. They took off on their honeymoon to a destination so secret, not even Holly knew where she was going—although she soon had an inkling.

It was a short flight and one that still brought back

some hair-raising memories, despite her having flown it with Brett several times since their plane had crashed. But, by the time they landed at the station Brett had bought for her as a wedding present, she'd long since been in no doubt as to where they were going.

This time they didn't ride the distance between the homestead and Tommy's Hut on a horse, they drove in a powerful, tough four-wheel-drive and reached their destination before sunset.

And there were other changes. Someone had been there before them. Someone had chopped the firewood and piled it up handily. Someone had provided camp chairs and a blow-up mattress. Someone had left an esky with champagne and foodstuffs in it.

All the same, Holly looked around with tears in her eyes, at the water lilies, the birds and the palms. 'I never, never thought I'd come back. Thank you.' She went into his arms.

'Did you like your wedding?' he enquired, holding her close.

'I loved it. How about you?'

'Same. Well,' he said after kissing her thoroughly, with a sudden little wicked glint in his eye, 'how about a swim, then a fish? We have two reels now, and I'm determined to out-fish you.'

Holly lifted her head from his shoulder. 'Oh! We'll see about that!'

But later, much later, when the fire had died down and they were lying in each other's arms, all forms of competitiveness had left them and they were awash with a lovely form of contentment.

'By the way,' he said, 'I thought two nights here, then

a trip to Africa. Or anywhere on earth you'd like to go, Mrs Wyndham.'

Holly breathed happily. 'I wondered when the mud hut and a herd of giraffe were going to make an appearance in my life!'

CHAPTER ELEVEN

Two years later they were sitting on a beach watching the moon rise and holding hands.

But this beach wasn't in the middle of nowhere; it was Palm Cove, and they'd come down from Haywire for a very important appointment.

It was a magic evening. The moon hung in the sky like a silver Christmas bauble. The sea was a slightly darker blue than the sky, apart from its ribbon of reflected moonlight, and you felt as if you could reach out and touch Double Island again.

It had been a magic two years since she'd married Brett Wyndham, Holly thought. Busy, productive and fulfilling.

His zoo was no longer a dream, it was a reality, and she'd taken part in a lot of the planning and the doing of it. Haywire was now very much home to her, although they spent time in Brisbane and they travelled extensively.

Yes, she conceded, there'd been some ups and downs—and she'd decided it was not possible to go through a marriage without them—but if anything they were growing ever closer.

And she felt confident that Brett had got over his fears that he was going down the path his father had trod.

Curiously, or perhaps not so curiously, it was her mother who'd put it into words only a few days ago.

When Holly had rung her full of delighted suspicions, Sylvia had said, 'You were right, darling—about Brett and believing in him.'

'You can tell now?' Holly had queried.

'Of course. Would you be so happy otherwise?'

'No.'

Now on the beach at Palm Cove, after an appointment in Cairns with a gynaecologist that had confirmed her pregnancy, Holly patted her stomach and said a little anxiously, 'Are you really thrilled at this news?'

'Of course.' He released her hand and put his arm round her shoulders. 'Why wouldn't I be? I like kids, and our kids will be special.'

She smiled, but it faded. 'But it means—it does mean we'll be tied down a bit. You see, I've got the feeling I'm going to be a pretty hands-on mother, and that will cut down on travelling and so on.'

'Holly.' Brett put his hands on her shoulders and turned her to face him. 'When will you accept that it's where *you* are that counts for me? Nothing else.'

And he stared down into the deep blue of her eyes with complete concentration in his own.

'Still? I mean, it hasn't worn off a bit or…?'

'Still. Always,' he said very quietly. 'Don't doubt it, Holly.'

She breathed deeply and went into his arms.

MODERN

NICOLO: THE POWERFUL SICILIAN
by Sandra Marton

She knew the Orsini name meant danger, but Alessia Antoninni was unprepared for Nicolo Orsini's lethal good looks. Soon, dangerously close to giving in to his demands, her heart *and* her business are at risk...

SHOCK: ONE-NIGHT HEIR
by Melanie Milburne

Giorgio Sabbatini must maintain the family line. Unable to give him an heir, wife Maya knows she has to walk away. But she can't resist one last night of passion...

HER LAST NIGHT OF INNOCENCE
by India Grey

After a near-fatal crash, racing driver Cristiano Maresca lost his memory. Now Kate Edwards must tell Italy's most notorious playboy he has a love-child!

BUTTONED-UP SECRETARY, BRITISH BOSS
by Susanne James

Alexander McDonald finds his new secretary Sabrina Gold tantalising. Having vowed never to mix business and pleasure, he's suddenly tempted to break his own rules...

On sale from 3rd December 2010
Don't miss out!

Available at WHSmith, Tesco, ASDA, Eason and all good bookshops

www.millsandboon.co.uk

MODERN

NAÏVE BRIDE, DEFIANT WIFE
by Lynne Graham

Alejandro Vasquez has never forgotten—nor forgiven—his runaway wife. When he discovers Jemima's whereabouts, and that he has a son, he'll settle the score…

STRANDED, SEDUCED…PREGNANT
by Kim Lawrence

The brooding Italian Severo Constanza comes to Neve Macleod's rescue knowing nothing of her scandalous past—just that he will delight in taking her as his own!

INNOCENT VIRGIN, WILD SURRENDER
by Anne Mather

On a quest to find her mother, Rachel Claiborne is distracted by the irresistible Matt Brody, who is clearly keeping secrets. Rachel must *not* give in to temptation…

CAPTURED AND CROWNED
by Janette Kenny

When Kristo Stanrakis takes his brother's fiancée for his queen, he realises Demetria is the unforgettable stranger with whom, years ago, he nearly made love. Now the king is determined to finish what he started!

On sale from 19th November 2010
Don't miss out!

Available at WHSmith, Tesco, ASDA, Eason and all good bookshops

www.millsandboon.co.uk

MILLS & BOON®
HAVE JOINED FORCES WITH THE LEANDER TRUST AND LEANDER CLUB TO HELP TO DEVELOP TOMORROW'S CHAMPIONS

ALL PROCEEDS TO THE LEANDER TRUST

We have produced a stunning calendar for 2011 featuring a host of Olympic and World Champions (as they've never been seen before!). Leander Club is recognised the world over for its extraordinary rowing achievements and is committed to developing its squad of athletes to help underpin future British success at World and Olympic level.

'All my rowing development has come through the support and back-up from Leander. The Club has taken me from a club rower to an Olympic Silver Medallist. Leander has been the driving force behind my progress'

RIC EGINGTON – Captain, Leander Club Olympic Silver, Beijing, 2009 World Champion.

Please send me ☐ calendar(s) @ £8.99 each plus £3.00 P&P (FREE postage and packing on orders of 3 or more calendars despatching to the same address).

I enclose a cheque for £ _____ made payable to Harlequin Mills & Boon Limited.

Name _____

Address _____

_____ Post code _____

Email _____

Send this whole page and cheque to:
Leander Calendar Offer
Harlequin Mills & Boon Limited
Eton House, 18-24 Paradise Road, Richmond TW9 1SR

All proceeds from the sale of the 2011 Leander Fundraising Calendar will go towards the Leander Trust (Registered Charity No: 284631) – and help in supporting aspiring athletes to train to their full potential.

MILLS & BOON®

are proud to present our...

Book of the Month

The Accidental Princess
by Michelle Willingham
from Mills & Boon® Historical

Etiquette demands Lady Hannah Chesterfield ignore
the shivers of desire Lieutenant Michael Thorpe's
wicked gaze provokes, but her unawakened body
clamours for his touch… So she joins Michael on
an adventure to uncover the secret of his birth—
is this common soldier really a prince?

Available 5th November

Something to say about our Book of the Month?
Tell us what you think!

millsandboon.co.uk/community
facebook.com/romancehq
twitter.com/millsandboonuk

THE

Balfour

LEGACY

Eight sisters, Eight scandals

VOLUME 5 – OCTOBER 2010
Zoe's Lesson
by Kate Hewitt

VOLUME 6 – NOVEMBER 2010
Annie's Secret
by Carole Mortimer

VOLUME 7 – DECEMBER 2010
Bella's Disgrace
by Sarah Morgan

VOLUME 8 – JANUARY 2011
Olivia's Awakening
by Margaret Way

8 VOLUMES IN ALL TO COLLECT!

/M&B/RTL3

Discover Pure Reading Pleasure with

**Visit the Mills & Boon website for all
the latest in romance**

- **Buy** all the latest releases, backlist and eBooks

- **Find out** more about our authors and their books

- **Join** our community and chat to authors and other readers

- **Free** online reads from your favourite authors

- **Win** with our fantastic online competitions

- **Sign** up for our free monthly eNewsletter

- **Tell us** what you think by signing up to our reader panel

- **Rate** and review books with our star system

www.millsandboon.co.uk

Follow us at twitter.com/millsandboonuk

Become a fan at facebook.com/romancehq

2 FREE BOOKS
AND A SURPRISE GIFT

We would like to take this opportunity to thank you for reading this Mills & Boon® book by offering you the chance to take TWO more specially selected books from the Modern™ series absolutely FREE! We're also making this offer to introduce you to the benefits of the Mills & Boon® Book Club™—

- **FREE home delivery**
- **FREE gifts and competitions**
- **FREE monthly Newsletter**
- **Exclusive Mills & Boon Book Club offers**
- **Books available before they're in the shops**

Accepting these FREE books and gift places you under no obligation to buy, you may cancel at any time, even after receiving your free books. Simply complete your details below and return the entire page to the address below. You don't even need a stamp!

YES Please send me 2 free Modern books and a surprise gift. I understand that unless you hear from me, I will receive 4 superb new books every month for just £3.30 each, postage and packing free. I am under no obligation to purchase any books and may cancel my subscription at any time. The free books and gift will be mine to keep in any case.

Ms/Mrs/Miss/Mr _____ Initials _____

Surname _____

Address _____

_____

_____ Postcode _____

E-mail _____

Send this whole page to: Mills & Boon Book Club, Free Book Offer, FREEPOST NAT 10298, Richmond, TW9 1BR

Offer valid in UK only and is not available to current Mills & Boon Book Club subscribers to this series. Overseas and Eire please write for details.. We reserve the right to refuse an application and applicants must be aged 18 years or over. Only one application per household. Terms and prices subject to change without notice. Offer expires 31st January 2011. As a result of this application, you may receive offers from Harlequin Mills & Boon and other carefully selected companies. If you would prefer not to share in this opportunity please write to The Data Manager, PO Box 676, Richmond, TW9 1WU.

Mills & Boon® is a registered trademark owned by Harlequin Mills & Boon Limited.
Modern™ is being used as a trademark. The Mills & Boon® Book Club™ is being used as a trademark.